THE RUSKIN BOND
CHILDREN'S OMNIBUS

An Original Rupa Paperback

Fifth impression 1997

Published 1994 by

Rupa & Co

15 Bankim Chatterjee Street, Calcutta 700 073
135 South Malaka, Allahabad 211 001
P.G. Solanki Path, Lamington Road, Bombay 400 007
7/16 Ansari Road, Daryaganj, New Delhi 110 002

Typeset in Baskerville by
Megatechnics
19A Ansari Road
New Delhi 110 002

Printed in India by
Gopsons Papers Ltd
A-28, Sector IX
Noida 201 301

Rs. 95

ISBN 81-7167-288-4

THE RUSKIN BOND
CHILDREN'S OMNIBUS

Rupa & Co

Dedicated

to the hundreds of readers, young and old,
who have written me such kind letters
over the years. . .

May you prosper and be happy!

Contents

Foreword	xi
Cricket for the Crocodile	1
The Blue Umbrella	19
Ghost Trouble	59
Angry River	83
Dust on the Mountain	129
Grandfather's Private Zoo	155
The Road to the Bazaar	207

Foreword

Ruskin Bond began writing when he was still in his teens, and he made his way without "introduction" from the great and the famous. With his gift for going straight to the heart of the reader, he had no need of an intermediary apart from his publisher.

During the last twenty years, Ruskin Bond has probably spent more time writing for children than for adults. Those who have grown up on his stories read them again as adults, and find that they are as fresh and enjoyable as ever. They then give his books to their own children. Ruskin Bond has long since broken the age barrier.

In this omnibus collection, Rupa presents some of his longer and most memorable stories — the epic Angry River, the lyrical Blue Umbrella, the exciting and realistic Dust on the Mountain. Sita battles the forces of nature. Binya has to overcome greed and stupidity. Bisnu is confronted by man's tendency to exploit and destroy his own natural heritage.

These are powerful stories — classics of their kind.

But there is also a lighter side to Bond, and he is at his humorous best in his "Grandfather" stories, especially those in which a large variety of pets take on the humans in the household and generally get the better of them. There is also a crocodile who disrupts a cricket match, and a mischievous ghost who adopts a family and plays havoc with their lives. And the charming children whose exploits are recorded in The Road to the Bazaar round off a collection that brings the young reader the best from "the man with the golden pen".

K.K.

Cricket for the Crocodile

One

Ranji was up at dawn.

It was Sunday, a school holiday. Although he was supposed to be preparing for his exams, only a fortnight away, he couldn't resist one or two more games before getting down to history and algebra and other unexciting things.

"I'm going to be a Test cricketer when I grow up," he told his mother. "Of what use will maths be to me?"

"You never know," said his mother, who happened to be more of a cricket fan than his father. "You might need maths to work out your batting average. And as for history, wouldn't you like to be a part of history? Famous cricketers make history!"

"Making history is all right," said Ranji. "As long as I don't have to remember the date on which I make it!"

*

Ranji met his friends and teammates in the park. The grass was still wet with dew, the sun only just rising behind the distant hills. The park was full of flower-beds, and

3

swings and slides for smaller children. The boys would have to play on the river bank against their rivals, the village boys. Ranji did not have a full team that morning, but he was looking for a "friendly" match. The really important game would be held the following Sunday.

The village team was quite good because the boys lived near each other and practised a lot together, whereas Ranji's team was drawn from all parts of the town. There was the baker's boy, Nathu; the tailor's son, Sunder; the postmaster's son, Prem; and the bank manager's son, Anil. These were some of the better players. Sometimes their fathers also turned up for a game. The fathers weren't very good, but you couldn't tell them that. After all, they helped to provide bats and balls and pocket-money.

A regular spectator at these matches was Nakoo the crocodile, who lived in the river. Nakoo means Nosey, but the village boys were very respectful and called him Nakoo-ji, Nakoo, sir. He had a long snout, rows of ugly-looking teeth (some of them badly in need of fillings), and a powerful scaly tail.

He was nearly fifteen feet long, but you did not see much of him; he swam low in the water and glided smoothly through the tall grasses near the river. Sometimes he came out on the river bank to bask in the sun. He did not care for people, especially cricketers. He disliked the noise they made, frightening away the water-birds and other creatures required for an interesting menu, and it was also alarming to have cricket balls plopping around in the shallows where he liked to rest.

Once Nakoo crept quite close to the bank manager, who was resting against one of the trees near the river bank. The bank manager was a portly gentleman, and Nakoo seemed to think he would make a good meal. Just then a party of villagers had come along, beating drums for a marriage party. Nakoo retired to the muddy waters of the river. He was a little tired of swallowing frogs, eels and herons. That juicy bank manager would make a nice change — he'd grab him one day!

*

The village boys were a little bigger than Ranji and his friends, but they did not bring their fathers along. The game made very little sense to the older villagers. And when balls came flying across fields to land in milk pails or cooking pots, they were as annoyed as the crocodile.

Today, the men were busy in the fields, and Nakoo the crocodile was wallowing in the mud behind a screen of reeds and water-lilies. How beautiful and innocent those lilies looked! Only sharp eyes would have noticed Nakoo's long snout thrusting above the broad flat leaves of the lilies. His eyes were slits. He was watching.

Ranji struck the ball hard and high. Splash! It fell into the river about thirty feet from where Nakoo lay. Village boys and town boys dashed into the shallow water to look for the ball. Too many of them! Crowds made Nakoo nervous. He slid away, crossed the river to the opposite bank, and sulked.

As it was a warm day, nobody seemed to want to get out of the water. Several boys threw off their clothes, deciding that it was a better day for swimming than for cricket. Nakoo's mouth watered as he watched those bare limbs splashing about.

"We're supposed to be practising," said Ranji, who took his cricket seriously. "We won't win next week."

"Oh, we'll win easily," said Anil joining him on the river bank. "My father says he's going to play."

"The last time he played, we lost," said Ranji. "He made two runs and forgot to field."

"He was out of form," said Anil, ever loyal to his father, the bank manager.

Sheroo, the captain of the village team, joined them. "My cousin from Delhi is going to play for us. He made a hundred in one of the matches there."

"He won't make a hundred on this wicket," said Ranji. "It's slow at one end and fast at the other."

"Can I bring my father?" asked Nathu, the baker's son. "Can he play?"

"Not too well, but he'll bring along a basket of biscuits, buns and pakoras."

"Then he can play," said Ranji, always quick to make up his mind. No wonder he was the team's captain! "If there are too many of us, we'll make him twelfth man."

The ball could not be found, and as they did not want to risk their spare ball, the practice session was declared over.

"My grandfather's promised me a new ball," said little Mani, from the village team, who bowled tricky leg-breaks which bounced off to the side.

"Does he want to play, too?" asked Ranji.

7

"No, of course not. He's nearly eighty."

"That's settled then," said Ranji. "We'll all meet here at nine o'clock next Sunday. Fifty overs a side."

They broke up, Sheroo and his team wandering back to the village, while Ranji and his friends got onto their bicycles (two or three to a bicycle, since not everyone had one), and cycled back to town.

Nakoo, left in peace at last, returned to his favourite side of the river and crawled some way up the river bank, as if to inspect the wicket. It had been worn smooth by the players, and looked like a good place to relax. Nakoo moved across it. He felt pleasantly drowsy in the warm sun, so he closed his eyes for a little nap. It was good to be out of the water for a while.

*

The following Sunday morning, a cycle bell tinkled at the gate. It was Nathu, waiting for Ranji to join him. Ranji hurried out of the house, carrying his bat and a thermos of lime juice thoughtfully provided by his mother.

"Have you got the stumps?" he asked.

"Sunder has them."

"And the ball?"

"Yes. And Anil's father is bringing one too, provided he opens the batting!"

Nathu rode, while Ranji sat on the cross bar with bat and thermos. Anil was waiting for them outside his house.

"My father's gone ahead on his scooter. He's picking up Nathu's father. I'll follow with Prem and Sunder."

Most of the boys got to the river bank before the bank

manager and the baker. They left their bicycles under a shady banyan tree and ran down the gentle slope to the river. And then, one by one, they stopped, astonished by what they saw.

They gaped in awe at their cricket pitch.

Across it, basking in the soft warm sunshine, was Nakoo the crocodile.

"Where did it come from?" asked Ranji.

"Usually he stays in the river," said Sheroo, who had joined them. "But all this week he's been coming out to lie on our wicket. I don't think he wants us to play."

"We'll have to get him off," said Ranji.

"You'd better keep out of reach of his tail and jaws!"

"We'll wait until he goes away," said Prem.

But Nakoo showed no signs of wanting to leave. He rather liked the smooth flat stretch of ground which he had discovered. And here were all the boys again, doing their best to disturb him.

After some time the boys began throwing pebbles at Nakoo. These had no effect, simply bouncing off the crocodile's tough hide. They tried mud balls and an orange. Nakoo twitched his tail and opened one eye, but refused to move on.

Then Prem took a ball, and bowled a fast one at the crocodile. It bounced just short of Nakoo and caught him on the snout. Startled and stung, he wriggled off the pitch and moved rapidly down the river bank and into the water. There was a mighty splash as he dived for cover.

"Well bowled, Prem!" said Ranji. "That was a good ball."

"Nakoo-ji will be in a bad mood after that," warned Sheroo. "Don't get too close to the river."

The bank manager and the baker were the last to arrive. The scooter had given them some trouble. No one mentioned the crocodile, just in case the adults decided to call the match off.

After inspecting the wicket, which Nakoo had left in fair condition, Sheroo and Ranji tossed a coin. Ranji called "Heads!" but it came up tails. Sheroo chose to bat first.

*

The tall Delhi player came out to open the innings with little Mani.

Mani was a steady bat, who could stay at the wicket for a long time; but in a one-day match, quick scoring was needed. This the Delhi player provided. He struck a four, then took a single off the last ball of the over.

In the third over, Mani tried to hit out and was bowled for a duck. So the village team's score was 13 for 1.

"Well done," said Ranji to fast bowler Prem. "But we'll have to get that tall fellow out soon. He seems quite good."

The tall fellow showed no sign of getting out. He hit two more boundaries and then swung one hard and high towards the river.

Nakoo, who had been sulking in the shallows, saw the ball coming towards him. He opened his jaws wide, and with a satisfying "clunk!" the ball lodged between his back teeth.

Nakoo got his teeth deep into the cricket ball and chewed. Revenge was sweet. And the ball tasted good, too. The combination of leather and cork was just right. Nakoo decided that he would snap up any other balls that came his way.

"Harmless old reptile," said the bank manager. He produced a new ball and insisted that he bowl with it.

It proved to be the most expensive over of the match. The bank manager's bowling was quite harmless and the Delhi player kept hitting the ball into the fields for fours and sixes. The score soon mounted to 40 for 1. The bank manager modestly took himself off.

By the time the tenth over had been bowled, the score had mounted to 70. Then Ranji, bowling slow spins, lost his grip on the ball and sent the batsman a full toss. Having played the good balls perfectly, the Delhi player couldn't resist taking a mighty swipe at the bad ball. He mistimed his shot and was astonished to see the ball fall into the hands of a fielder near the boundary. 70 for 2. The game was far from being lost for Ranji's team.

A couple of wickets fell cheaply, and then Sheroo came in and started playing rather well. His drives were straight and clean. The ball cut down the buttercups and hummed over the grass. A big hit landed in a poultry yard. Feathers flew and so did curses. Nakoo raised his head to see what all the noise was about. No further cricket balls came his way, and he gazed balefully at a heron who was staying just out of his reach.

The score mounted steadily. The fielding grew slack, as it often does when batsmen gain the upper hand. A catch was dropped. And Nathu's father, keeping wicket, missed a stumping chance.

"No more grown-ups in our team," grumbled Nathu.

The baker made amends by taking a good catch behind the wicket. The score was 115 for 5, with about half the overs remaining.

Sheroo kept his end up, but the remaining batsmen struggled for runs and the end came with about 5 overs still to go. A modest total of 145.

"Should be easy," said Ranji.

"No problem," said Prem.

"Lunch first," said the bank manager, and they took a half-hour break.

The village boys went to their homes for rest and refreshment, while Ranji and his team spread themselves out under the banyan tree.

Nathu's father had brought patties and pakoras: the bank manager brought a basket of oranges and bananas; Prem had brought a jack-fruit curry; Ranji had brought a halwa made from carrots, milk and sugar; Sunder had brought a large container full of savoury rice cooked with peas and fried onions; and the others had brought various curries, pickles and sauces. Everything was shared, and with the picnic in full swing no one noticed that Nakoo the crocodile had left the water. Using some tall reeds as cover, he had crept half way up the river bank. Those delicious food smells had reached him too, and he was unwilling to be left out of the picnic. Perhaps the boys would leave something for him. If not....

"Time to start," announced the bank manager, getting

up. "I'll open the batting. We need a good start if we are going to win!

*

The bank manager strode out to the wicket in the company of young Nathu. Sheroo opened the bowling for the village team.

The bank manager took a run off the first ball. He puffed himself up and waved his bat in the air as though the match had already been won. Nathu played out the rest of the over without taking any chances.

The tall Delhi player took up the bowling from the other end. The bank manager tapped his bat impatiently, then raised it above his shoulders, ready to hit out. The bowler took a long fast run up to the bowling crease. He gave a little leap, his arm swung over, and the ball came at the bank manager in a swift, curving flight.

The bank manager still had his bat raised when the ball flew past him and uprooted his middle stump.

A shout of joy went up from the fielders. The bank manager was on his way back to the shade of the banyan tree.

"A fly got in my eye," he muttered. "I wasn't ready. Flies everywhere!" And he swatted angrily at flies that no one else could see.

The villagers, hearing that someone as important as a bank manager was in their midst, decided that it would be wrong for him to sit on the ground like everyone else. So they brought him a cot from the village. It was one of those light wooden beds, taped with strands of thin rope.

13

The bank manager lowered himself into it rather gingerly. It creaked but took his weight.

The score was 1 for 1.

Anil took his father's place at the wicket and scored ten runs in two overs. The bank manager pretended not to notice but he was really quite pleased. "Takes after me," he said, and made himself comfortable on the cot.

Nathu kept his end up while Anil scored the runs. Then Anil was out, skying a catch to mid wicket.

25 for 2 in six overs. It could have been worse.

"Well played!" called the bank manager to his son, and then lost interest in the proceedings. He was soon fast asleep on the cot. The flies did not seem to bother him any more.

Nathu kept going, and there were a couple of good partnerships for the fourth and fifth wickets. When the Delhi player finished his share of overs, the batsmen became more free in their stroke-play. Then little Mani got a ball to spin sharply, and Nathu was caught by the wicket-keeper.

It was 75 for 4 when Ranji came in to bat.

Before he could score a run, his partner at the other end was bowled. And then Nathu's father strode up to the wicket, determined to do better than the bank manager. In this he succeeded by one run.

The baker scored two, and then in trying to run another two when there was only one to be had, found himself stranded halfway up the wicket. The wicket-keeper knocked his stumps down.

The boys were too polite to say anything. And as for the

bank manager he was now fast asleep under the banyan tree.

So intent was everyone on watching the cricket that no one noticed that Nakoo the crocodile had crept further up the river bank to slide beneath the cot on which the bank manager was sleeping.

There was just room enough for Nakoo to get between the legs of the cot. He thought it was a good place to lie concealed, and he seemed not to notice the large man sleeping peacefully just above him.

Soon the bank manager was snoring gently, and it was not long before Nakoo dozed off, too. Only, instead of snoring, Nakoo appeared to be whistling through his crooked teeth.

*

75 for 5 and it looked as though Ranji's team would soon be crashing to defeat.

Sunder joined Ranji and, to everyone's delight, played two lovely drives to the boundary. Then Ranji got into his stride and cut and drove the ball for successive fours. The score began to mount steadily. 112 for 5. Once again there were visions of victory.

After Sunder was out, stumped, Ranji was joined by Prem, a big hitter. Runs came quickly. The score reached 140. Only six runs were needed for victory.

Ranji decided to do it in style. Receiving a half-volley, he drove the ball hard and high towards the banyan tree.

Thump! It struck Nakoo on the jaw and loosened one of his teeth.

It was the second time that day he'd been caught napping. He'd had enough of it.

Nakoo lunged forward, tail thrashing and jaws snapping. The cot, with the manager still on it, rose with him. Crocodile and cot were now jammed together, and when Nakoo rushed forward, he took the cot with him.

The bank manager, dreaming that he was at sea in a rowing boat, woke up to find the cot pitching violently from side to side.

"Help!" he shouted. "Help!"

The boys scattered in all directions, for the crocodile was now advancing down the wicket, knocking over stumps and digging up the pitch. He found an abandoned sun hat and swallowed it. A wicket-keeper's glove went the same way. A batsman's pad was caught up on his tail.

All this time the bank manager hung on to the cot for safety, but would he be able to get out of reach of Nakoo's jaw and tail? He decided to hang on to the cot until it was dislodged.

"Come on, boys, help!" he shouted. "Get me off!"

But the cot remained firmly attached to the crocodile, and so did the bank manager.

The problem was solved when Nakoo made for the river and plunged into its familiar waters. Then the bank manager tumbled into the water and scrambled up the bank, while Nakoo made for the opposite shore.

The bank manager's ordeal was over, and so was the cricket match.

"Did you see how I dealt with that crocodile?" he said,

still dripping, but in a better humour now that he was safe again "By the way, who won the match?"

"We don't know," said Ranji, as they trudged back to their bicycles. "That would have been a six if you hadn't been in the way."

Sheroo, who had accompanied them as far as the main road, offered a return match the following week.

"I'm busy next week," said the baker.

"I have another game," said the bank manager.

"What game is that, sir?" asked Ranji.

"Chess," said the bank manager.

Ranji and his friends began making plans for the next match.

"You won't win without us," said the bank manager.

"Not a chance," said the baker.

But Ranji's team did, in fact, win the next match.

Nakoo the crocodile did not trouble them, because the cot was still attached to his back, and it took him several weeks to get it off.

A number of people came to the river bank to look at the crocodile who carried his own bed around.

Some even stayed to watch the cricket.

The Blue Umbrella

One

"Neelu! Neelu!" cried Binya.

She scrambled barefoot over the rocks, ran over the short summer grass, up and over the brow of the hill, all the time calling "Neelu, Neelu!"

Neelu — Blue — was the name of the blue-grey cow. The other cow, which was white, was called Gori, meaning Fair One. They were fond of wandering off on their own, down to the stream or into the pine forest, and sometimes they came back by themselves and sometimes they stayed away — almost deliberately, it seemed to Binya.

If the cows didn't come home at the right time, Binya would be sent to fetch them. Sometimes her brother Bijju went with her, but these days he was busy preparing for his exams and didn't have time to help with the cows.

Binya liked being on her own, and sometimes she allowed the cows to lead her into some distant valley, and then they would all be late coming home. The cows preferred having Binya with them, because she let them wander. Bijju pulled them by their tails if they went too far.

21

Binya belonged to the mountains, to this part of the Himalayas known as Garhwal. Dark forests and lonely hilltops held no terrors for her. It was only when she was in the market-town, jostled by the crowds in the bazaar, that she felt rather nervous and lost. The town, five miles from the village, was also a pleasure resort for tourists from all over India.

Binya was probably ten. She may have been nine or even eleven, she couldn't be sure because no one in the village kept birthdays; but her mother told her she'd been born during a winter when the snow had come up to the windows, and that was just over ten years ago, wasn't it? Two years later her father had died; but his passing away had made no difference to their way of life. They had three tiny terraced fields on the side of the mountain, and they grew potatoes, onions, ginger, beans, mustard and maize: not enough to sell in the town, but enough to live on.

Like most mountain girls, Binya was quite sturdy, fair of skin, with pink cheeks and dark eyes and her black hair tied in a pigtail. She wore pretty glass bangles on her wrists, and a necklace of glass beads. From the necklace hung a leopard's claw. It was a lucky charm, and Binya always wore it. Bijju had one, too, only his was attached to a string.

Binya's full name was Binyadevi, and Bijju's real name was Vijay, but everyone called them Binya and Bijju. Binya was two years younger than her brother.

She had stopped calling for Neelu; she had heard the cow-bells tinkling, and knew the cows hadn't gone far.

Singing to herself, she walked over fallen pine-needles into the forest glade on the spur of the hill. She heard voices, laughter, the clatter of plates and cups; and stepping through the trees, she came upon a party of picnickers.

They were holiday-makers from the plains. The women were dressed in bright saris, the men wore light summer shirts, and the children had pretty new clothes. Binya, standing in the shadows between the trees, went unnoticed; and for some time she watched the picnickers, admiring their clothes, listening to their unfamiliar accents, and gazing rather hungrily at the sight of all their food. And then her gaze came to rest on a bright blue umbrella, a frilly thing for women, which lay open on the grass beside its owner.

Now Binya had seen umbrellas before, and her mother had a big black umbrella which nobody used any more because the field-rats had eaten holes in it, but this was the first time Binya had seen such a small, dainty, colourful umbrella; and she fell in love with it. The umbrella was like a flower, a great blue flower that had sprung up on the dry brown hillside.

She moved forward a few paces so that she could see the umbrella better. As she came out of the shadows into the sunlight, the picnickers saw her.

"Hello, look who's here!" exclaimed the older of the two women. "A little village girl!"

"Isn't she pretty?" remarked the other. "But how torn and dirty her clothes are!" It did not seem to bother them that Binya could hear and understand everything they said about her.

"They're very poor in the hills," said one of the men.

"Then let's give her something to eat." And the older woman beckoned to Binya to come closer.

Hesitantly, nervously, Binya approached the group. Normally she would have turned and fled; but the attraction was the pretty blue umbrella. It had cast a spell over her, drawing her forward almost against her will.

"What's that on her neck?" asked the younger woman.

"A necklace of sorts."

"It's a pendant — see, there's a claw hanging from it!"

"It's a tiger's claw," said the man beside her. (He had never seen a tiger's claw.) "A lucky charm. These people wear them to keep away evil spirits." He looked to Binya for confirmation, but Binya said nothing.

"Oh, I want one too!" said the woman, who was obviously his wife.

"You can't get them in shops."

"Buy hers, then. Give her two or three rupees, she's sure to need the money."

The man, looking slightly embarrassed but anxious to please his young wife, produced a two-rupee note and offered it to Binya, indicating that he wanted the pendant in exchange. Binya put her hand to the necklace, half afraid that the excited woman would snatch it away from her. Solemnly she shook her head. The man then showed her a five-rupee note, but again Binya shook her head.

"How silly she is!" exclaimed the young woman.

"It may not be hers to sell," said the man. "But I'll try again. How much do you want — what can we give you?"

And he waved his hand towards the picnic things scattered about on the grass.

Without any hesitation Binya pointed to the umbrella.

"My umbrella!" exclaimed the young woman. "She wants my umbrella. What cheek!"

"Well, you want her pendant, don't you?"

"That's different."

"Is it?"

The man and his wife were beginning to quarrel with each other.

"I'll ask her to go away," said the older woman. "We're making such fools of ourselves."

"But I *want* the pendant!" cried the other petulantly. And then, on an impulse, she picked up the umbrella and held it out to Binya. "Here, take the umbrella!"

Binya removed her necklace and held it out to the young woman, who immediately placed it round her own neck. Then Binya took the umbrella and held it up. It did not look so small in her hands; in fact, it was just the right size.

She had forgotten about the picnickers, who were busy examining the pendant. She turned the blue umbrella this way and that; looked through the bright blue silk at the pulsating sun; and then, still keeping it open, turned and disappeared into the forest glade.

Two

Binya seldom closed the blue umbrella. Even when she had it in the house, she left it lying open in a corner of the room. Sometimes Bijju snapped it shut, complaining that it got in the way. She would open it again a little later. It wasn't beautiful when it was closed.

Whenever Binya went out — whether it was to graze the cows, or fetch water from the spring, or carry milk to the little tea shop on the Tehri road — she took the umbrella with her. That patch of skyblue silk could always be seen on the hillside.

Old Ram Bharosa (Ram the Trustworthy) kept the tea shop on the Tehri road. It was a dusty, unmetalled road. Once a day, the Tehri bus stopped near his shop and passengers got down to sip hot tea or drink a glass of curds. He kept a few bottles of Coca-cola too; but as there was no ice, the bottles got hot in the sun and so were seldom opened. He also kept sweets and toffees, and when Binya or Bijju had a few coins to spare they would spend them at the shop. It was only a mile from the village.

Ram Bharosa was astonished to see Binya's blue umbrella.

"What have you there, Binya?" he asked.

Binya gave the umbrella a twirl and smiled at Ram Bharosa. She was always ready with her smile, and would willingly have lent it to anyone who was feeling unhappy.

"That's a lady's umbrella," said Ram Bharosa. "That's only for Mem-Sahibs. Where did you get it?"

"Someone gave it to me — for my necklace."

"You exchanged it for your lucky claw!"

Binya nodded.

"But what do you need it for? The sun isn't hot enough — and it isn't meant for the rain. It's just a pretty thing for rich ladies to play with!"

Binya nodded and smiled again. Ram Bharosa was quite right; it was just a beautiful plaything. And that was exactly why she had fallen in love with it.

"I have an idea," said the shopkeeper.

"It's no use to you, that umbrella. Why not sell it to me? I'll give you five rupees for it."

"It's worth fifteen," said Binya.

"Well, then, I'll give you ten."

Binya laughed and shook her head.

"Twelve rupees?" said Ram Bharosa, but without much hope.

Binya placed a five-paisa coin on the counter. "I came for a toffee," she said.

Ram Bharosa pulled at his drooping whiskers, gave Binya a wry look, and placed a toffee in the palm of her hand. He watched Binya as she walked away along the

30

dusty road. The blue umbrella held him fascinated, and he stared after it until it was out of sight.

The villagers used this road to go to the market-town. Some used the bus; a few rode on mules; most people walked. Today, everyone on the road turned their heads to stare at the girl with the bright blue umbrella.

Binya sat down in the shade of a pine tree. The umbrella, still open, lay beside her. She cradled her head in her arms, and presently she dozed off. It was that kind of day, sleepily warm and summery.

And while she slept, a wind sprang up.

It came quietly, swishing gently through the trees, humming softly. Then it was joined by other random gusts, bustling over the tops of the mountains. The trees shook their heads and came to life. The wind fanned Binya's cheeks. The umbrella stirred on the grass.

The wind grew stronger, picking up dead leaves and sending them spinning and swirling through the air. It got into the umbrella and began to drag it over the grass. Suddenly it lifted the umbrella and carried it about six feet from the sleeping girl. The sound woke Binya.

She was on her feet immediately, and then she was leaping down the steep slope. But just as she was within reach of the umbrella, the wind picked it up again and carried it further downhill.

Binya set off in pursuit. The wind was in a wicked, playful mood. It would leave the umbrella alone for a few moments; but, as soon as Binya came near, it would pick up the umbrella again and send it bouncing, floating, dancing away from her.

The hill grew steeper. Binya knew that after twenty yards it would fall away in a precipice. She ran faster. And the wind ran with her, ahead of her, and the blue umbrella stayed up with the wind.

A fresh gust picked it up and carried it to the very edge of the cliff. There it balanced for a few seconds, before toppling over, out of sight.

Binya ran to the edge of the cliff. Going down on her hands and knees, she peered down the cliff-face. About a hundred feet below, a small stream rushed between great boulders. Hardly anything grew on the cliff-face — just a few stunted bushes, and, half way down, a wild cherry tree growing crookedly out of the rocks and hanging across the chasm. The umbrella had stuck in the cherry tree.

Binya didn't hesitate. She may have been timid with strangers, but she was at home on a hillside. She stuck her bare leg over the edge of the cliff and began climbing down. She kept her face to the hillside, feeling her way with her feet, only changing her handhold when she knew her feet were secure. Sometimes she held on to the thorny bilberry bushes, but she did not trust the other plants, which came away very easily.

Loose stones rattled down the cliff. Once on their way, the stones did not stop until they reached the bottom of the hill; and they took other stones with them, so that there was soon a cascade of stones, and Binya had to be very careful not to start a landslide.

As agile as a mountain-goat, she did not take more than five minutes to reach the crooked cherry tree. But the

most difficult task remained. She had to crawl along the trunk of the tree, which stood out at right angles from the cliff. Only by doing this could she reach the trapped umbrella.

Binya felt no fear when climbing trees. She was proud of the fact that she could climb them as well as Bijju. Gripping the rough cherry bark with her toes, and using her knees as leverage, she crawled along the trunk of the projecting tree until she was almost within reach of the umbrella. She noticed with dismay that the blue cloth was torn in a couple of places.

She looked down; and it was only then that she felt afraid. She was right over the chasm, balanced precariously about eighty feet above the blouder-strewn stream. Looking down, she felt quite dizzy. Her hands shook, and the tree shook too. If she slipped now, there was only one direction in which she could fall — down, down, into the depths of that dark and shadowy ravine.

There was only one thing to do; concentrate on the patch of blue just a couple of feet away from her.

She did not look down or up, but straight ahead; and willing herself forward, she managed to reach the umbrella.

She could not crawl back with it in her hands. So, after dislodging it from the forked branch in which it had stuck, she let it fall, still open, into the ravine below.

Cushioned by the wind, the umbrella floated serenely downwards, landing in a thicket of nettles.

Binya crawled back along the trunk of the cherry tree.

Twenty minutes later she emerged from the nettle

clump, her precious umbrella held aloft. She had nettle stings all over her legs, but she was hardly aware of the smarting. She was as immune to nettles as Bijju was to bees.

By following the course of the stream, Binya found a narrow goat-track and another, easier way home.

Three

About four years previously, Bijju had knocked a hive out of an oak tree, and had been badly stung about the face and legs. It had been a painful experience. But now, if a bee stung him, he felt nothing at all: he had been immunised for life!

He was on his way home from school. It was two o'clock and he hadn't eaten since six in the morning. Fortunately, the Kingora bushes — the bilberries — were in fruit, and already Bijju's lips were stained purple with the juice of the wild, sour fruit.

He didn't have any money to spend at Ram Bharosa's shop, but he stopped there anyway, to look at the sweets in their glass jars.

"And what will you have today?" asked Ram Bharosa.

"No money," said Bijju.

"You can pay me later."

Bijju shook his head. Some of his friends had taken sweets on credit, and at the end of the month they had found they'd eaten more sweets than they could possibly pay for! As a result, they'd had to hand over to Ram

Bharosa some of their most treasured possessions — such as a curved knife for cutting grass, or a small hand-axe, or a jar for pickles, or a pair of earrings — and these had become the shopkeeper's possessions and were kept by him or sold in his shop.

Ram Bharosa had set his heart on having Binya's blue umbrella, and so naturally he was anxious to give credit to either of the children; but so far neither had fallen into the trap.

Bijju moved on, his mouth full of Kingora berries. Half way home, he saw Binya with the cows. It was late evening, and the sun had gone down, but Binya still had the umbrella open. The two small rents had been stitched up by her mother.

Bijju gave his sister a handful of berries. She handed him the umbrella while she ate the berries.

"You can have the umbrella until we get home," she said. It was her way of rewarding Bijju for bringing her the wild fruit.

Calling "Neelu! Gori!" Binya and Bijju set out for home, followed at some distance by the cows.

It was dark before they reached the village, but Bijju still had the umbrella open.

*

Most of the people in the village were a little envious of Binya's blue umbrella. No one else had ever possessed one like it. The schoolmaster's wife thought it was quite wrong for a poor cultivator's daughter to have such a fine umbrella while she, a second-class B.A., had to make do

37

with an ordinary black one. Her husband offered to have their old umbrella dyed blue; she gave him a scornful look, and loved him a little less than before. The Pujari, who looked after the temple, announced that he would buy a multi-coloured umbrella the next time he was in the town. A few days later he returned, looking annoyed and grumbling that they weren't available except in Delhi. Most people consoled themselves by saying that Binya's pretty umbrella wouldn't keep out the rain, if it rained heavily; that it would shrivel in the sun, if the sun was fierce; that it would collapse in a wind, if the wind was strong; that it would attract lightning, if lightning fell near it; and that it would prove unlucky, if there was any ill-luck going about. Secretly, everyone admired it.

Unlike the adults, the children didn't have to pretend. They were full of praise for the umbrella. It was so light, so pretty, so bright a blue! And it was just the right size for Binya. They knew that if they said nice things about the umbrella, Binya would smile and give it to them to hold for a little while — just a very little while!

Soon it was the time of the monsoon. Big black clouds kept piling up, and thunder rolled over the hills.

Binya sat on the hillside all afternoon, waiting for the rain. As soon as the first big drop of rain came down, she raised the umbrella over her head. More drops, big ones, came pattering down. She could see them through the umbrella silk, as they broke against the cloth.

And then there was a cloudburst, and it was like standing under a waterfall. The umbrella wasn't really a rain-umbrella, but it held up bravely. Only Binya's feet got wet. Rods of rain fell around her in a curtain of shivered glass.

Everywhere on the hillside people were scurrying for shelter. Some made for a charcoal-burner's hut; others for a mule-shed, or Ram Bharosa's shop. Binya was the only one who didn't run. This was what she'd been waiting for — rain on her umbrella — and she wasn't in a hurry to go home. She didn't mind getting her feet wet. The cows didn't mind getting wet, either.

Presently she found Bijju sheltering in a cave. He would have enjoyed getting wet, but he had his school books with him and he couldn't afford to let them get spoilt. When he saw Binya, he came out of the cave and shared the umbrella. He was a head taller than his sister, so he had to hold the umbrella for her, while she held his books.

The cows had been left far behind.

"Neelu, Neelu!" called Binya.

"Gori!" called Bijju.

When their mother saw them sauntering home through the driving rain, she called out: "Binya! Bijju! Hurry up, and bring the cows in! What are you doing out there in the rain?"

"Just testing the umbrella," said Bijju.

Four

The rains set in, and the sun only made brief appearances. The hills turned a lush green. Ferns sprang up on walls and tree-trunks. Giant lilies reared up like leopards from the tall grass. A white mist coiled and uncoiled as it floated up from the valley. It was a beautiful season, except for the leeches.

Every day, Binya came home with a couple of leeches fastened to the flesh of her bare legs. They fell off by themselves just as soon as they'd had their thimbleful of blood; but you didn't know they were on you until they fell off; and then, later, the skin became very sore and itchy. Some of the older people still believed that to be bled by leeches was a remedy for various ailments. Whenever Ram Bharosa had a headache, he applied a leech to his throbbing temple.

Three days of incessant rain had flooded out a number of small animals who lived in holes in the ground. Binya's mother suddenly found the roof full of field-rats. She had to drive them out; they ate too much of her stored-up wheat flour and rice. Bijju liked lifting up large rocks, to disturb the scorpions who were sleeping beneath. And snakes came out to bask in the sun.

Binya had just crossed the small stream at the bottom of the hill when she saw something gliding out of the bushes and coming towards her. It was a long black snake. A clatter of loose stones frightened it. Seeing the girl in its way, it rose up, hissing, prepared to strike. The forked tongue darted out, the venomous head lunged at Binya.

Binya's umbrella was open as usual. She thrust it forward, between herself and the snake, and the snake's hard snout thudded twice against the strong silk of the umbrella. The reptile then turned and slithered away over the wet rocks, disappearing in a clump of ferns.

Binya forgot about the cows and ran all the way home to tell her mother how she had been saved by the umbrella. Bijju had to put away his books and go out to fetch the cows. He carried a stout stick, in case he met with any snakes.

*

First the summer sun, and now the endless rain, meant that the umbrella was beginning to fade a little. From a bright blue it had changed to a light blue. But it was still a pretty thing, and tougher than it looked, and Ram Bharosa still desired it. He did not want to sell it; he wanted to own it. He was probably the richest man in the area — so why shouldn't he have a blue umbrella? Not a day passed without his getting a glimpse of Binya and the umbrella; and the more he saw the umbrella, the more he wanted it.

43

The schools closed during the monsoon, but this didn't mean that Bijju could sit at home doing nothing. Neelu and Gori were providing more milk than was required at home, so Binya's mother was able to sell a kilo of milk every day: half a kilo to the schoolmaster, and half a kilo (at reduced rate) to the temple Pujari. Bijju had to deliver the milk every morning.

Ram Bharosa had asked Bijju to work in his shop during the holidays, but Bijju didn't have time; he had to help his mother with the ploughing and the transplanting of the rice-seedlings. So Ram Bharosa employed a boy from the next village, a boy called Rajaram. He did all the washing-up, and ran various errands. He went to the same school as Bijju, but the two boys were not friends.

One day, as Binya passed the shop, twirling her blue umbrella, Rajaram noticed that his employer gave a deep sigh and began muttering to himself.

"What's the matter, Babuji?" asked the boy.

"Oh, nothing," said Ram Bharosa. "It's just a sickness that has come upon me. And it's all due to that girl Binya and her wretched umbrella."

"Why, what has she done to you?"

"Refused to sell me her umbrella! There's pride for you. And I offered her ten rupees."

"Perhaps, if you gave her twelve..."

"But it isn't new any longer. It isn't worth eight rupees now. All the same, I'd like to have it."

"You wouldn't make a profit on it," said Rajaram.

"It's not the profit I'm after, wretch! It's the thing itself. It's the beauty of it!"

"And what would you do with it, Babuji? You don't visit anyone — you're seldom out of your shop. Of what use would it be to you?"

"Of what use is a poppy in a cornfield? Of what use is a rainbow? Of what use are you, numbskull? Wretch! I, too, have a soul. I want the umbrella, because — because I want its beauty to be mine!"

Rajaram put the kettle on to boil, began dusting the counter, all the time muttering: "I'm as useful as an umbrella," and then, after a short period of intense thought, said: "What will you give me, Babuji, if I get the umbrella for you?"

"What do you mean?" asked the old man.

"You know what I mean. What will you give me?"

"You mean to steal it, don't you, you wretch? What a delightful child you are! I'm glad you're not my son or my enemy. But look — everyone will know it has been stolen, and then how will I be able to show off with it?"

"You will have to gaze upon it in secret," said Rajaram with a chuckle. "Or take it into Tehri, and have it coloured red! That's your problem. But tell me, Babuji, do you want it badly enough to pay me three rupees for stealing it without being seen?"

Ram Bharosa gave the boy a long, sad look. "You're a sharp boy," he said. "You'll come to a bad end. I'll give you two rupees."

"Three," said the boy.

"Two," said the old man.

"You don't really want it, I can see that," said the boy.

"Wretch!" said the old man. "Evil one! Darkener of my

doorstep! Fetch me the umbrella, and I'll give you three rupees."

Five

Binya was in the forest glade where she had first seen the umbrella. No one came there for picnics during the monsoon. The grass was always wet and the pine-needles were slippery underfoot. The tall trees shut out the light, and poisonous-looking mushrooms, orange and purple, sprang up everywhere. But it was a good place for porcupines, who seemed to like the mushrooms; and Binya was searching for porcupine-quills.

The hill people didn't think much of porcupine-quills, but far away in southern India the quills were valued as charms and sold at a rupee each. So Ram Bharosa paid a tenth of a rupee for each quill brought to him, and he in turn sold the quills at a profit to a trader from the plains.

Binya had already found five quills, and she knew there'd be more in the long grass. For once, she'd put her umbrella down. She had to put it aside if she was to search the ground thoroughly.

It was Rajaram's chance.

He'd been following Binya for some time, concealing himself behind trees and rocks, creeping closer whenever she became absorbed in her search. He was anxious that she should not see him and be able to recognize him later.

He waited until Binya had wandered some distance from the umbrella. Then, running forward at a crouch, he seized the open umbrella and dashed off with it.

But Rajaram had very big feet. Binya heard his heavy footsteps and turned just in time to see him as he disappeared between the trees. She cried out, dropped the porcupine-quills, and gave chase.

Binya was swift and sure-footed, but Rajaram had a long stride. All the same, he made the mistake of running downhill. A long-legged person is much faster going up hill than down. Binya reached the edge of the forest glade in time to see the thief scrambling down the path to the stream. He had closed the umbrella so that it would not hinder his flight.

Binya was beginning to gain on the boy. He kept to the path, while she simply slid and leapt down the steep hillside. Near the bottom of the hill the path began to straighten out, and it was here that the long-legged boy began to forge ahead again.

Bijju was coming home from another direction. He had a bundle of sticks which he'd collected for the kitchen fire. As he reached the path, he saw Binya rushing down the hill as though all the mountain-spirits in Garhwal were after her.

"What's wrong?" he called. "Why are you running?"

Binya paused only to point at the fleeing Rajaram.

"My umbrella!" she cried. "He has stolen it!"

Bijju dropped his bundle of sticks, and ran after his sister. When he reached her side, he said, "I'll soon catch him!" and went sprinting away over the lush green grass. He was fresh, and he was soon well ahead of Binya and gaining on the thief.

Rajaram was crossing the shallow stream when Bijju caught up with him. Rajaram was the taller boy, but Bijju was much stronger. He flung himself at the thief, caught him by the legs, and brought him down in the water. Rajaram got to his feet, and tried to drag himself away; but Bijju still had him by a leg. Rajaram overbalanced and came down with a great splash. He had let the umbrella fall. It began to float away on the current. Just then Binya arrived, flushed and breathless, and went dashing into the stream after the umbrella.

Meanwhile, a tremendous fight was taking place. Locked in fierce combat, the two boys swayed together on a rock, tumbled on to the sand, rolled over and over the pebbled bank until they were again threshing about in the shallows of the stream. The magpies, bulbuls and other birds were disturbed, and flew away with cries of alarm.

Covered with mud, gasping and spluttering, the boys groped for each other in the water. After five minutes of frenzied struggle, Bijju emerged victorious. Rajaram lay flat on his back on the sand, exhausted, while Bijju sat astride him, pinning him down with his arms and legs.

"Let me get up!" gasped Rajaram. "Let me go — I don't want your useless umbrella!"

"Then why did you take it?" demanded Bijju. "Come

on — tell me why!"

"It was that skinflint Ram Bharosa," said Rajaram. "He told me to get it for him. He said if I didn't fetch it, I'd lose my job."

Six

By early October the rains were coming to an end. The leeches disappeared. The ferns turned yellow, and the sunlight on the green hills was mellow and golden, like the limes on the small tree in front of Binya's home. Bijju's days were happy ones, as he came home from school, munching on roasted corn. Binya's umbrella had turned a pale milky blue, and was patched in several places, but it was still the prettiest umbrella in the village, and she still carried it with her wherever she went.

The cold, cruel winter wasn't far off, but somehow October seems longer than other months, because it is a kind month: the grass is good to lie upon, the breeze is warm and gentle and pine-scented. That October everyone seemed contented — everyone, that is, except Ram Bharosa.

The old man had by now given up all hope of ever possessing Binya's umbrella. He wished he had never set eyes on it. Because of the umbrella he had suffered the tortures of greed, the despair of loneliness. Because of the umbrella, people had stopped coming to his shop!

Ever since it had become known that Ram Bharosa had tried to have the umbrella stolen, the village people had turned against him. They stopped trusting the old man, instead of buying their soap and tea and matches from his shop, they preferred to walk an extra mile to the shops near the Tehri bus stand. Who would have dealings with a man who had sold his soul for an umbrella? The children taunted him, twisted his name around. From "Ram the Trustworthy" he became "Trusty Umbrella Thief".

The old man sat alone in his empty shop, listening to the eternal hissing of his kettle, and wondering if anyone would ever again step in for a glass of tea. Ram Bharosa had lost his own appetite, and ate and drank very little. There was no money coming in. He had his savings in a bank in Tehri, but it was a terrible thing to have to dip into them! To save money, he had dismissed the blundering Rajaram. So he was left without any company. The roof leaked, and the wind got in through the corrugated tin sheets, but Ram Bharosa didn't care.

Bijju and Binya passed his shop almost every day. Bijju went by with a loud but tuneless whistle. He was one of the world's whistlers; cares rested lightly on his shoulders. But, strangely enough, Binya crept quietly past the shop, looking the other way, almost as though she was in some way responsible for the misery of Ram Bharosa.

She kept reasoning with herself, telling herself that the umbrella was her very own, and that she couldn't help it if others were jealous of it. But had she loved the umbrella too much? Had it mattered more to her than people mattered? She couldn't help feeling that in a small way

53

she was the cause of the sad look on Ram Bharosa's face ("His face is a yard long," said Bijju) and the ruinous condition of his shop. It was all due to his own greed, no doubt; but she didn't want him to feel too bad about what he'd done, because it made her feel bad about herself; and so she closed the umbrella whenever she came near the shop, opening it again only when she was out of sight.

One day towards the end of October, when she had ten paise in her pocket, she entered the shop and asked the old man for a toffee.

She was Ram Bharosa's first customer in almost two weeks. He looked suspiciously at the girl. Had she come to taunt him, to flaunt the umbrella in his face? She had placed her coin on the counter. Perhaps it was a bad coin. Ram Bharosa picked it up and bit it; he held it up to the light; he rang it on the ground. It was a good coin. He gave Binya the toffee.

Binya had already left the shop when Ram Bharosa saw the closed umbrella lying on his counter. There it was, the blue umbrella he had always wanted, within his grasp at last! He had only to hide it at the back of his shop, and no one would know that he had it, no one could prove that Binya had left it behind.

He stretched out his trembling, bony hand, and took the umbrella by the handle. He pressed it open. He stood beneath it, in the dark shadows of his shop, where no sun or rain could ever touch it.

"But I'm never in the sun or in the rain," he said aloud. "Of what use is an umbrella to me?"

And he hurried outside and ran after Binya.

54

"Binya, Binya!" he shouted. "Binya, you've left your umbrella behind!"

He wasn't used to running, but he caught up with her, held out the umbrella, saying, "You forgot it — the umbrella!"

In that moment it belonged to both of them.

But Binya didn't take the umbrella. She shook her head and said, "You keep it. I don't need it any more."

"But it's such a pretty umbrella!" protested Ram Bharosa. "It's the best umbrella in the village."

"I know," said Binya. "But an umbrella isn't everything."

And she left the old man holding the umbrella, and went tripping down the road, and there was nothing between her and the bright blue sky.

Seven

Well, now that Ram Bharosa has the blue umbrella — a gift from Binya, as he tells everyone — he is sometimes persuaded to go out into the sun or the rain, and as a result he looks much healthier. Sometimes he uses the umbrella to chase away pigs or goats. It is always left open outside the shop, and anyone who wants to borrow it may do so; and so in a way it has become everyone's umbrella. It is faded and patchy, but it is still the best umbrella in the village.

People are visiting Ram Bharosa's shop again. Whenever Bijju or Binya stop for a cup of tea, he gives them a little extra milk or sugar. They like their tea sweet and milky.

A few nights ago, a bear visited Ram Bharosa's shop. There had been snow on the higher ranges of the Himalayas, and the bear had been finding it difficult to obtain food; so it had come lower down, to see what it could pick up near the village. That night it scrambled on to the tin roof of Ram Bharosa's shop, and made off with a huge pumpkin which had been ripening on the roof. But

56

in climbing off the roof, the bear had lost a claw.

Next morning Ram Bharosa found the claw just outside the door of his shop. He picked it up and put it in his pocket. A bear's claw was a lucky find.

A day later, when he went into the market-town, he took the claw with him, and left it with a silversmith, giving the craftsman certain instructions.

The silversmith made a locket for the claw; then he gave it a thin silver chain. When Ram Bharosa came again, he paid the silversmith ten rupees for his work.

The days were growing shorter, and Binya had to be home a little earlier every evening. There was a hungry leopard at large, and she couldn't leave the cows out after dark.

She was hurrying past Ram Bharosa's shop when the old man called out to her.

"Binya, spare a minute! I want to show you something."

Binya stepped into the shop.

"What do you think of it?" asked Ram Bharosa, showing her the silver pendant with the claw.

"It's so beautiful," said Binya, just touching the claw and the silver chain.

"It's a bear's claw," said Ram Bharosa. "That's even luckier than a leopard's claw. Would you like to have it?"

"I have no money," said Binya.

"That doesn't matter. You gave me the umbrella — I give you the claw! Come, let's see what it looks like on you."

He placed the pendant on Binya, and indeed it looked

very beautiful on her.

Ram Bharosa says he will never forget the smile she gave him when she left the shop.

She was half way home when she realized she had left the cows behind.

"Neelu, Neelu!" she called. "Oh, Gori!"

There was a faint tinkle of bells as the cows came slowly down the mountain path.

In the distance she could hear her mother and Bijju calling for her.

She began to sing. They heard her singing, and knew she was safe and near.

She walked home through the darkening glade, singing of the stars; and the trees stood still and listened to her, and the mountains were glad.

Ghost Trouble

One

It was Grandfather who finally decided that we would have to move to another house.

And it was all because of a Pret, a mischievous north Indian ghost, who had been making life difficult for everyone.

Prets usually live in peepul trees, and that's where our little ghost first had his home — in the branches of a massive old peepul tree which had grown through the compound wall and spread into our garden. Part of the tree was on our side of the wall, part on the other side, shading the main road. It gave the ghost a good view of the whole area.

For many years the Pret had lived there quite happily, without bothering anyone in our house. It did not bother me, either, and I spent a lot of time in the peepul tree. Sometimes I went there to escape the adults at home, sometimes to watch the road and the people who passed by. The peepul tree was cool on a hot day, and the heart-shaped leaves were always revolving in the breeze. This constant movement of the leaves also helped to disguise

the movements of the Pret, so that I never really knew exactly where he was sitting. But he paid no attention to me. The traffic on the road kept him fully occupied.

Sometimes, when a tonga was passing, he would jump down and frighten the pony, and as a result the little pony-cart would go rushing off in the wrong direction.

Sometimes he would get into the engine of a car or a bus, which would have a breakdown soon afterwards.

And he liked to knock the sun-helmets off the heads of sahibs or officials, who would wonder how a strong breeze had sprung up so suddenly, only to die down just as quickly. Although this special kind of ghost could make himself felt, and sometimes heard, he was invisible to the human eye.

I was not invisible to the human eye, and often got the blame for some of the Pret's pranks. If bicycle-riders were struck by mango seeds or apricot stones, they would look up, see a small boy in the branches of the tree, and threaten me with terrible consequences. Drivers who went off after parking their cars in the shade would sometimes come back to find their tyres flat. My protests of innocence did not carry much weight. But when I mentioned the Pret in the tree, they would look uneasy, either because they thought I must be mad, or because they were afraid of ghosts, especially Prets. They would find other things to do and hurry away.

At night no one walked beneath the peepul tree.

It was said that if you yawned beneath the tree, the Pret would jump down your throat and give you a pain. Our gardener, Chandu, who was always taking sick-leave, blamed the Pret for his tummy troubles. Once, when yawning, Chandu had forgotten to put his hand in front of his mouth, and the ghost had got in without any trouble.

Now Chandu spent most of his time lying on a string-bed in the courtyard of his small house. When Grandmother went to visit him, he would start groaning and holding his sides, the pain was so bad; but when she went away, he did not fuss so much. He claimed that the pain did not affect his appetite, and he ate a normal diet, in fact a little more than normal — the extra amount was meant to keep the ghost happy!

Two

"Well, it isn't our fault," said Grandfather, who had given permission to the Public Works Department to cut the tree, which had been on our land. They wanted to widen the road, and the tree and a bit of our wall were in the way. So both had to go.

Several people protested, including the Raja of Jinn, who lived across the road and who sometimes asked Grandfather over for a game of tennis.

"That peepul tree has been there for hundreds of years," he said. "Who are we to cut it down?"

"*We,*" said the Chief Engineer, "are the P.W.D."

And not even a ghost can prevail against the wishes of the Public Works Department.

They brought men with saws and axes, and first they lopped all the branches until the poor tree was quite naked. It must have been at this moment that the Pret moved out. Then they sawed away at the trunk until, finally, the great old peepul came crashing down on the road, bringing down the telephone wires and an electric pole in the process, and knocking a large gap in the Raja's

65

garden wall.

It took them three days to clear the road, and during that time the Chief Engineer swallowed a lot of dust and tree-pollen. For months afterwards he complained of a choking feeling, although no doctor could ever find anything in his throat.

"It's the Pret's doing," said the Raja knowingly. "They should never have cut that tree."

Deprived of his tree, the Pret decided that he would live in our house.

I first became aware of his presence when I was sitting on the verandah steps, reading a book. A tiny chuckling sound came from behind me. I looked round, but no one was to be seen. When I returned to my book, the chuckling started again. I paid no attention. Then a shower of rose petals fell softly on to the pages of my open book. The Pret wanted me to know he was there!

"All right," I said. "So you've come to stay with us. Now let me read."

He went away then; but as a good Pret has to be bad in order to justify his existence, it was not long before he was up to all sorts of mischief.

He began by hiding Grandmother's spectacles.

"I'm sure I put them down on the dining-table," she grumbled.

A little later they were found balanced on the snout of a wild boar, whose stuffed and mounted head adorned the verandah wall, a memento of Grandfather's hunting trips when he was young.

66

Naturally, I was at first blamed for this prank. But a day or two later, when the spectacles disappeared again, only to be found dangling from the bars of the parrot's cage, it was agreed that I was not to blame; for the parrot had once bitten off a piece of my finger, and I did not go near it any more.

The parrot was hanging upside down, trying to peer through one of the lenses. I don't know if they improved his vision, but what he saw certainly made him angry, because the pupils of his eyes went very small and he dug his beak into the spectacle frames, leaving them with a permanent dent. I caught them just before they fell to the floor.

But even without the help of the spectacles, it seemed that our parrot could see the Pret. He would keep turning this way and that, lunging out at unseen fingers, and protecting his tail from the tweaks of invisible hands. He had always refused to learn to talk, but now he became quite voluble and began to chatter in some unknown tongue, often screaming with rage and rolling his eyes in a frenzy.

"We'll have to give that parrot away," said Grandmother. "He gets more bad-tempered by the day."

Grandfather was the next to be troubled.

He went into the garden one morning to find all his prize sweet-peas broken off and lying on the grass. Chandu thought the sparrows had destroyed the flowers, but we didn't think the birds could have finished off every single bloom just before sunrise.

"It must be the Pret," said Grandfather, and I agreed.

The Pret did not trouble me much, because he remembered me from his peepul-tree days and knew I resented the tree being cut as much as he did. But he liked to catch my attention, and he did this by chuckling and squeaking near me when I was alone, or whispering in my ear when I was with someone else. Gradually I began to make out the occasional word. He had started learning English!

Three

Uncle Benji, who came to stay with us for long periods when he had little else to do (which was most of the time), was soon to suffer.

He was a heavy sleeper, and once he'd gone to bed he hated being woken up. So when he came to breakfast looking bleary-eyed and miserable, we asked him if he was feeling all right.

"I couldn't sleep a wink last night," he complained. "Whenever I was about to fall asleep, the bedclothes would be pulled off the bed. I had to get up at least a dozen times to pick them off the floor." He stared suspiciously at me. "Where were *you* sleeping last night, young man?"

"In Grandfather's room," I said. "I've lent you *my* room."

"It's that ghost from the peepul tree," said Grandmother with a sigh.

"Ghost!" exclaimed Uncle Benji. "I didn't know the house was haunted."

"It is now," said Grandmother. "First my spectacles,

then the sweet-peas, and now Benji's bedclothes! What will it be up to next, I wonder?"

We did not have to wonder for long.

There followed a series of minor disasters. Vases fell off tables, pictures fell from walls. Parrots' feathers turned up in the teapot, while the parrot himself let out indignant squawks and swear-words in the middle of the night. Windows which had been closed would be found open, and open windows closed.

Finally, Uncle Benji found a crow's nest in his bed, and on tossing it out of the window was attacked by two crows.

Then Aunt Ruby came to stay, and things quietened down for a time.

Did Aunt Ruby's powerful personality have an effect on the Pret, or was he just sizing her up?

"I think the Pret has taken a fancy to your aunt," said Grandfather mischievously. "He's behaving himself for a change."

This may have been true, because the parrot, who had picked up some of the English words being tried out by the Pret, now called out, "*Kiss, kiss,*" whenever Aunt Ruby was in the room.

"What a charming bird," said Aunt Ruby.

"You can keep him if you like," said Grandmother.

One day Aunt Ruby came in to the house covered in rose petals.

"I don't know where they came from," she exclaimed. "I was sitting in the garden, drying my hair, when handfuls of petals came showering down on me!"

"It likes you," said Grandfather.

"What likes me?"

"The ghost."

"What ghost?"

"The Pret. It came to live in the house when the peepul tree was cut down."

"What nonsense!" said Aunt Ruby.

"*Kiss, kiss!*" screamed the parrot.

"There aren't any ghosts, Prets or other kinds," said Aunt Ruby firmly.

"*Kiss, kiss!*" screeched the parrot again. Or was it the parrot? The sound seemed to be coming from the ceiling.

"I wish that parrot would shut up."

"It isn't the parrot," I said. "It's the Pret."

Aunt Ruby gave me a cuff over the ear and stormed out of the room.

But she had offended the Pret. From being her admirer, he turned into her enemy. Somehow her toothpaste got switched with a tube of Grandfather's shaving-cream. When she appeared in the dining-room, foaming at the mouth, we ran for our lives, Uncle Benji shouting that she'd got rabies.

Four

Two days later Aunt Ruby complained that she had been struck on the nose by a grapefruit, which had leapt mysteriously from the pantry shelf and hurled itself at her.

"If Ruby and Benji stay here much longer, they'll both have nervous breakdowns," said Grandfather thoughtfully.

"I thought they broke down long ago," I said.

"None of your cheek," snapped Aunt Ruby.

"He's in league with that Pret to try and get us out of here," said Uncle Benji.

"Don't listen to him — you can stay as long as you like," said Grandmother, who never turned away any of her numerous nephews, nieces, cousins or distant relatives.

The Pret, however, did not feel so hospitable, and the persecution of Aunt Ruby continued.

"When I looked in the mirror this morning," she complained bitterly, "I saw a little monster, with huge ears, bulging eyes, flaring nostrils and a toothless grin!"

"You don't look *that* bad, Aunt Ruby," I said, trying to be nice.

"It was either you or that imp you call a Pret," said Aunt Ruby. "And if it's a ghost, then it's time we all moved to another house."

Uncle Benji had another idea.

"Let's drive the ghost out," he said. "I know a Sadhu who rids houses of evil spirits."

"But the Pret's not evil," I said. "Just mischievous."

Uncle Benji went off to the bazaar and came back a few hours later with a mysterious long-haired man who claimed to be a Sadhu — one who has given up all worldly goods, including most of his clothes.

He prowled about the house, and lighted incense in all the rooms, despite squawks of protest from the parrot. All the time he chanted various magic spells. He then collected a fee of thirty rupees, and promised that we would not be bothered again by the Pret.

As he was leaving, he was suddenly blessed with a shower — no, it was really a downpour — of dead flowers, decaying leaves, orange peel and banana skins. All spells forgotten, he ran to the gate and made for the safety of the bazaar.

Aunt Ruby declared that it had become impossible to sleep at night because of the devilish chuckling that came from beneath her pillow. She packed her bags and left.

Uncle Benji stayed on. He was still having trouble with his bedclothes, and he was beginning to talk to himself, which was a bad sign.

"Talking to the Pret, Uncle?" I asked innocently, when I caught him at it one day.

He gave me a threatening look. "What did you say?" he demanded. "Would you mind repeating that?"

I thought it safer to please him. "Oh, didn't you hear me?" I said, *Teaching the parrot, Uncle?*"

He glared at me, then walked off in a huff. If he did not leave it was because he was hoping Grandmother would lend him enough money to buy a motorcycle; but Grandmother said he ought to try earning a living first.

One day I found him on the drawing-room sofa, laughing like a madman. Even the parrot was so alarmed that it was silent, head lowered and curious. Uncle Benji was red in the face — literally red all over!

"What happened to your face, Uncle?" I asked.

He stopped laughing and gave me a long hard look. I realized that there had been no joy in his laughter.

"Who painted the wash-basin red without telling me?" he asked in a quavering voice.

As Uncle Benji looked really dangerous, I ran from the room.

"We'll have to move, I suppose," said Grandfather later. "Even if it's only for a couple of months. I'm worried about Benji. I've told him that I painted the wash-basin myself but forgot to tell him. He doesn't believe me. He thinks it's the Pret or the boy, or both of them! Benji needs a change. So do we. There's my brother's house at the other end of the town. He won't be using it for a few months. We'll move in next week."

And so, a few days and several disasters later, we began moving house.

Five

Two bullock-carts laden with furniture and heavy luggage were sent ahead. Uncle Benji went with them. The roof of our old car was piled high with bags and kitchen utensils. Grandfather took the wheel, I sat beside him, and Granny sat in state at the back.

We set off and had gone some way down the main road when Grandfather started having trouble with the steering-wheel. It appeared to have got loose, and the car began veering about on the road, scattering cyclists, pedestrians, and stray dogs, pigs and hens. A cow refused to move, but we missed it somehow, and then suddenly we were off the road and making for a low wall. Grandfather pressed his foot down on the brake, but we only went faster. "Watch out!" he shouted.

It was the Raja of Jinn's garden wall, made of single bricks, and the car knocked it down quite easily and went on through it, coming to a stop on the Raja's lawn.

"Now look what you've done," said Grandmother.

"Well, we missed the flower-beds," said Grandfather.

"Someone's been tinkering with the car. Our Pret, no doubt."

The Raja and two attendants came running towards us.

The Raja was a perfect gentleman, and when he saw that the driver was Grandfather, he beamed with pleasure.

"Delighted to see you, old chap!" he exclaimed. "Jolly decent of you to drop in. How about a game of tennis?"

"Sorry to have come in through the wall," apologized Grandfather.

"Don't mention it, old chap. The gate was closed, so what else could you do?"

Grandfather was as much of a gentleman as the Raja, so he thought it only fair to join him in a game of tennis. Grandmother and I watched and drank lemonade. After the game, the Raja waved us goodbye and we drove back through the hole in the wall and out on to the road. There was nothing much wrong with the car.

We hadn't gone far when we heard a peculiar sound, as of someone chuckling and talking to himself. It came from the roof of the car.

"Is the parrot out there on the luggage-rack?" asked Grandfather.

"No," said Grandmother. "He went ahead with Uncle Benji."

Grandfather stopped the car, got out, and examined the roof.

"Nothing up there," he said, getting in again and starting the engine. "I thought I heard the parrot."

When we had gone a little further, the chuckling

80

started again. A squeaky little voice began talking in English in the tones of the parrot.

"It's the Pret," whispered Grandmother. "What is he saying?"

The Pret's squeak grew louder. "Come on, come on!" he cried gleefully. "A new house! The same old friends! What fun we're going to have!"

Grandfather stopped the car. He backed into a driveway, turned round, and began driving back to our old house.

"What are you doing?" asked Grandmother.

"Going home," said Grandfather.

"And what about the Pret?"

"What about him? He's decided to live with us, so we'll have to make the best of it. You can't solve a problem by running away from it."

"All right," said Grandmother. "But what will we do about Benji?"

"It's up to him, isn't it? He'll be all right if he finds something to do."

Grandfather stopped the car in front of the verandah steps.

"I'm hungry," I said.

"It will have to be a picnic lunch," said Grandmother. "Almost everything was sent off on the bullock-carts."

As we got out of the car and climbed the verandah steps, we were greeted by showers of rose petals and sweet-scented jasmine.

"How lovely!" exclaimed Grandmother, smiling. "I think he likes us, after all."

Angry River

In the middle of the big river, the river that began in the mountains and ended in the sea, was a small island. The river swept round the island, sometimes clawing at its banks, but never going right over it. It was over twenty years since the river had flooded the island, and at that time no one had lived there. But for the last ten years a small hut had stood there, a mud-walled hut with a sloping thatched roof. The hut had been built into a huge rock, so only three of the walls were mud, and the fourth was rock.

Goats grazed on the short grass which grew on the island, and on the prickly leaves of thorn bushes. A few hens followed them about. There was a melon patch and a vegetable patch.

In the middle of the island stood a peepul tree. It was the only tree there.

Even during the Great Flood, when the island had been under water, the tree had stood firm.

It was an old tree. A seed had been carried to the island by a strong wind some fifty years back, had found shelter

between two rocks, had taken root there, and had sprung up to give shade and shelter to a small family; and Indians love peepul trees, especially during the hot summer months when the heart-shaped leaves catch the least breath of air and flutter eagerly, fanning those who sit beneath.

A sacred tree, the peepul: the abode of spirits, good and bad.

"Don't yawn when you are sitting beneath the tree," Grandmother used to warn Sita. "And if you must yawn, always snap your fingers in front of your mouth. If you forget to do that, a spirit might jump down your throat!"

"And then what will happen?" asked Sita.

"It will probably ruin your digestion," said Grandfather, who wasn't much of a believer in spirits.

The peepul had a beautiful leaf, and Grandmother likened it to the body of the mighty god Krishna — broad at the shoulders, then tapering down to a very slim waist.

It was an old tree, and an old man sat beneath it.

He was mending a fishing-net. He had fished in the river for ten years, and he was a good fisherman. He knew where to find the slim silver Chilwa fish and the big beautiful Mahseer and the long-moustached Singhara; he knew where the river was deep and where it was shallow; he knew which baits to use — which fish liked worms and which liked gram. He had taught his son to fish, but his son had gone to work in a factory in a city, nearly a hundred miles away. He had no grandson; but he had a grand-daughter, Sita, and she could do all the things a boy could do, and sometimes she could do them better.

She had lost her mother when she was very small. Grandmother had taught her all the things a girl should know, and she could do these as well as most girls. But neither of her grandparents could read or write, and as a result Sita couldn't read or write either.

There was a school in one of the villages across the river, but Sita had never seen it. There was too much to do on the island.

While Grandfather mended his net, Sita was inside the hut, pressing her Grandmother's forehead, which was hot with fever. Grandmother had been ill for three days and could not eat. She had been ill before, but she had never been so bad. Grandfather had brought her some sweet oranges from the market in the nearest town, and she could suck the juice from the oranges, but she couldn't eat anything else.

She was younger than Grandfather, but, because she was sick, she looked much older. She had never been very strong.

When Sita noticed that Grandmother had fallen asleep, she tip-toed out of the room on her bare feet, and stood outside.

The sky was dark with monsoon clouds. It had rained all night, and in a few hours it would rain again. The monsoon rains had come early, at the end of June. Now it was the middle of July, and already the river was swollen. Its rushing sound seemed nearer and more menacing than usual.

Sita went to her grandfather and sat down beside him beneath the peepul tree.

"When you are hungry, tell me," she said, "and I will make the bread."

"Is your grandmother asleep?"

"She sleeps. But she will wake soon, for she has a deep pain."

The old man stared out across the river, at the dark green of the forest, at the grey sky, and said, "Tomorrow, if she is not better, I will take her to the hospital at Shahganj. There they will know how to make her well. You may be on your own for a few days — but you have been on your own before..."

Sita nodded gravely; she had been alone before, even during the rainy season. Now she wanted Grandmother to get well, and she knew that only Grandfather had the skill to take the small dug-out boat across the river when the current was so strong. Someone would have to stay behind to look after their few possessions.

Sita was not afraid of being alone, but she did not like the look of the river. That morning, when she had gone down to fetch water, she had noticed that the level had risen. Those rocks which were normally spattered with the droppings of snipe and curlew and other water-birds had suddenly disappeared.

They disappeared every year — but not so soon, surely?

"Grandfather, if the river rises, what will I do?"

"You will keep to the high ground."

"And if the water reaches the high ground?"

"Then take the hens into the hut, and stay there."

"And if the water comes into the hut?"

"Then climb into the peepul tree. It is a strong tree. It

will not fall. And the water cannot rise higher than the tree!"

"And the goats, Grandfather?"

"I will be taking them with me, Sita. I may have to sell them, to pay for good food and medicines for your grandmother. As for the hens, if it becomes necessary, put them on the roof. But do not worry too much" — and he patted Sita's head — "the water will not rise as high. I will be back soon, remember that."

"And won't Grandmother come back?"

"Yes, of course — but they may keep her in the hospital for some time."

* * *

Towards evening it began to rain again, big pellets of rain, scarring the surface of the river. But it was warm rain, and Sita could move about in it. She was not afraid of getting wet, she rather liked it. In the previous month, when the first monsoon shower had arrived, washing the dusty leaves of the tree and bringing up the good smell of the earth, she had exulted in it, had run about shouting for joy. She was used to it now, and indeed a little tired of the rain, but she did not mind getting wet. It was steamy indoors, and her thin dress would soon dry in the heat from the kitchen fire.

She walked about barefooted, barelegged. She was very sure on her feet; her toes had grown accustomed to gripping all kinds of rocks, slippery or sharp. And though thin, she was surprisingly strong.

Black hair, streaming across her face. Black eyes. Slim

91

brown arms. A scar on her thigh: when she was small, visiting her mother's village, a hyaena had entered the house where she was sleeping, fastened on to her leg and tried to drag her away; but her screams had roused the villagers, and the hyaena had run off.

She moved about in the pouring rain, chasing the hens into a shelter behind the hut. A harmless brown snake, flooded out of its hole, was moving across the open ground. Sita picked up a stick, scooped the snake up, and dropped it between a cluster of rocks. She had no quarrel with snakes. They kept down the rats and the frogs. She wondered how the rats had first come to the island — probably in someone's boat, or in a sack of grain. Now it was a job to keep their numbers down.

When Sita finally went indoors, she was hungry. She ate some dried peas, and warmed up some goat's milk.

Grandmother woke once, and asked for water, and Grandfather held the brass tumbler to her lips.

*   *   *

It rained all night.

The roof was leaking, and a small puddle formed on the floor. They kept the kerosene-lamp alight. They did not need the light, but somehow it made them feel safer.

The sound of the river had always been with them, although they were seldom aware of it; but that night they noticed a change in its sound. There was something like a moan, like a wind in the tops of tall trees, and a swift hiss as the water swept round the rocks and carried away pebbles. And sometimes there was a rumble, as loose

92

earth fell into the water.

Sita could not sleep.

She had a rag doll, made with Grandmother's help out of bits of old clothing. She kept it by her side every night. The doll was someone to talk to, when the nights were long and sleep elusive. Her grandparents were often ready to talk, and Grandmother, when she was well, was a good story-teller; but sometimes Sita wanted to have secrets, and, though there were no special secrets in her life, she made up a few, because it was fun to have them. And if you have secrets, you must have a friend to share them with, a companion of one's own age. Since there were no other children on the island, Sita shared her secrets with the rag doll, whose name was Mumta.

Grandfather and Grandmother were asleep, though the sound of Grandmother's laboured breathing was almost as persistent as the sound of the river.

"Mumta," whispered Sita in the dark, starting one of her private conversations. "Do you think Grandmother will get well again?"

Mumta always answered Sita's questions, even though the answers could only be heard by Sita.

"She is very old," said Mumta.

"Do you think the river will reach the hut?" asked Sita.

"If it keeps raining like this, and the river keeps rising, it will reach the hut."

"I am a little afraid of the river, Mumta. Aren't you afraid?"

"Don't be afraid. The river has always been good to us."

94

"What will we do if it comes into the hut?"

"We will climb on the roof."

"And if it reaches the roof?"

"We will climb the peepul tree. The river has never gone higher than the peepul tree."

As soon as the first light showed through the little skylight, Sita got up and went outside. It wasn't raining hard, it was drizzling, but it was the sort of drizzle that could continue for days, and it probably meant that heavy rain was falling in the hills, where the river originated.

Sita went down to the water's edge. She couldn't find her favourite rock, the one on which she often sat dangling her feet in the water, watching the little Chilwa fish swim by. It was still there, no doubt, but the river had gone over it.

She stood on the sand, and she could feel the water oozing and bubbling beneath her feet.

The river was no longer green and blue and flecked with white, but a muddy colour.

She went back to the hut. Grandfather was up now. He was getting his boat ready.

Sita milked the goat. Perhaps it was the last time she would milk it.

*   *   *

The sun was just coming up when Grandfather pushed off in the boat. Grandmother lay in the prow. She was staring hard at Sita, trying to speak, but the words would not come. She raised her hand in a blessing.

Sita bent and touched her grandmother's feet, and

then Grandfather pushed off. The little boat — with its two old people and three goats — riding swiftly on the river, moved slowly, very slowly, towards the opposite bank. The current was so swift now, that Sita realized the boat would be carried about half-a-mile downstream before Grandfather could get it to dry land.

It bobbed about on the water, getting smaller and smaller, until it was just a speck on the broad river.

And suddenly Sita was alone.

There was a wind, whipping the rain-drops against her face; and there was the water, rushing past the island; and there was the distant shore, blurred by rain; and there was the small hut; and there was the tree.

Sita got busy. The hens had to be fed. They weren't bothered about anything except food. Sita threw them handfuls of coarse grain and potato-peelings and peanut-shells.

Then she took the broom and swept out the hut; lit the charcoal-burner, warmed some milk, and thought, "Tomorrow there will be no milk...." She began peeling onions. Soon her eyes started smarting, and, pausing for a few moments and glancing round the quiet room, she became aware again that she was alone. Grandfather's hookah-pipe stood by itself in one corner. It was a beautiful old hookah, which had belonged to Sita's great-grandfather. The bowl was made out of a coconut encased in silver. The long winding stem was at least four feet in length. It was their most valuable possession. Grandmother's sturdy Shisham-wood walking stick stood in another corner.

Sita looked around for Mumta, found the doll beneath the cot, and placed her within sight and hearing.

Thunder rolled down from the hills. BOOM — BOOM — BOOM....

"The gods of the mountains are angry," said Sita. "Do you think they are angry with me?"

"Why should they be angry with you?" asked Mumta.

"They don't have to have a reason for being angry. They are angry with everything, and we are in the middle of everything. We are so small — do you think they know we are here?"

"Who knows what the gods think?"

"But I made you," said Sita, "and I know you are here."

"And will you save me if the river rises?"

"Yes, of course. I won't go anywhere without you, Mumta."

Sita couldn't stay indoors for long. She went out, taking Mumta with her, and stared out across the river, to the safe land on the other side. But was it safe there? The river looked much wider now. Yes, it had crept over its banks and spread far across the flat plain. Far away, people were driving their cattle through waterlogged, flooded fields, carrying their belongings in bundles on their heads or shoulders, leaving their homes, making for the high land. It wasn't safe anywhere.

She wondered what had happened to Grandfather and Grandmother. If they had reached the shore safely, Grandfather would have to engage a bullock-cart, or a pony-drawn carriage, to get Grandmother to the district town, five or six miles away, where there was a market, a

court, a jail, a cinema, and a hospital.

She wondered if she would ever see Grandmother again. She had done her best to look after the old lady, remembering the times when Grandmother had looked after her, had gently touched her fevered brow, and had told her stories — stories about the gods — about the young Krishna, friend of birds and animals, so full of mischief, always causing confusion among the other gods; and Indra, who made the thunder and lightning; and Vishnu, the Preserver of all good things, whose steed was a great white bird; and Ganesh, with the elephant's head; and Hanuman, the monkey-god, who helped the young Prince Rama in his war with the King of Ceylon. Would Grandmother return to tell her more about them — or would she have to find out for herself?

The island looked much smaller now. In parts, the mud banks had dissolved quickly, sinking into the river. But in the middle of the island there was rocky ground, and the rocks would never crumble, they could only be submerged. In a space in the middle of the rocks grew the tree.

Sita climbed into the tree to get a better view. She had climbed the tree many times, and it took her only a few seconds to reach the higher branches. She put her hand to her eyes to shield them from the rain, and gazed upstream.

There was water everywhere. The world had become one vast river. Even the trees on the forested side of the river looked as though they had grown from the water, like mangroves. The sky was banked with massive,

moisture-laden clouds. Thunder rolled down from the hills, and the river seemed to take it up with a hollow booming sound.

Something was floating down with the current, something big and bloated. It was closer now, and Sita could make out the bulky object — a drowned buffalo — being carried rapidly downstream.

So the water had already inundated the villages further upstream. Or perhaps the buffalo had been grazing too close to the rising river.

Sita's worst fears were confirmed when, a little later, she saw planks of wood, small trees and bushes, and then a wooden bedstead, floating past the island.

How long would it take for the river to reach her own small hut?

As she climbed down from the tree, it began to rain more heavily. She ran indoors, shooing the hens before her. They flew into the hut and huddled under Grandmother's cot. Sita thought it would be best to keep them together now. And having them with her took away some of the loneliness.

There were three hens and a cock bird. The river did not bother them. They were interested only in food, and Sita kept them happy by throwing them a handful of onion-skins.

She would have liked to close the door and shut out the swish of the rain and the boom of the river; but then she would have no way of knowing how fast the water rose.

She took Mumta in her arms, and began praying for the rain to stop and the river to fall. She prayed to the

102

god Indra, and, just in case he was busy elsewhere, she prayed to other gods too. She prayed for the safety of her grandparents and for her own safety. She put herself last but only with great difficulty.

She would have to make herself a meal. So she chopped up some onions, fried them, then added turmeric and red chilli-powder and stirred until she had everything sizzling; then she added a tumbler of water, some salt, and a cup of one of the cheaper lentils. She covered the pot and allowed the mixture to simmer.

Doing this took Sita about ten minutes. It would take at least half-an-hour for the dish to be ready.

When she looked outside, she saw pools of water amongst the rocks and near the tree. She couldn't tell if it was rain-water or overflow from the river.

She had an idea.

A big tin trunk stood in a corner of the room. It had belonged to Sita's mother. There was nothing in it except a cotton-filled quilt, for use during the cold weather. She would stuff the trunk with everything useful or valuable, and weigh it down so that it wouldn't be carried away — just in case the river came over the island....

Grandfather's hookah went into the trunk. Grandmother's walking-stick went in, too. So did a number of small tins containing the spices used in cooking — nutmeg, caraway seed, cinnamon, coriander and pepper — and a bigger tin of flour and a tin of raw sugar. Even if Sita had to spend several hours in the tree, there would be something to eat when she came down again.

A clean white cotton shirt of Grandfather's, and

Grandmother's only spare sari also went into the trunk. Never mind if they got stained with yellow curry powder! Never mind if they got to smell of salted fish — some of that went in, too.

Sita was so busy packing the trunk that she paid no attention to the lick of cold water at her heels. She locked the trunk, placed the key high on the rock-wall, and turned to give her attention to the lentils. It was only then that she discovered that she was walking about on a watery floor.

She stood still, horrified by what she saw. The water was oozing over the threshold, pushing its way into the room.

Sita was filled with panic. She forgot about her meal and everything else. Darting out of the hut, she ran splashing through ankle-deep water towards the safety of the peepul tree. If the tree hadn't been there, such a well-known landmark, she might have floundered into deep water, into the river.

She climbed swiftly into the strong arms of the tree, made herself secure on a familiar branch, and thrust the wet hair away from her eyes.

* * *

She was glad she had hurried. The hut was now surrounded by water. Only the higher parts of the island could still be seen — a few rocks, the big rock into which the hut was built, a hillock on which some thorny bilberry bushes grew.

The hens hadn't bothered to leave the hut. They were probably perched on the cot now.

104

Would the river rise still higher? Sita had never seen it like this before. It swirled around her, stretching away in all directions.

More drowned cattle came floating down. The most unusual things went by on the water — an aluminium kettle, a cane-chair, a tin of tooth-powder, an empty cigarette packet, a wooden slipper, a plastic doll....

A doll!

With a sinking feeling, Sita remembered Mumta.

Poor Mumta! She had been left behind in the hut. Sita, in her hurry, had forgotten her only companion.

Well, thought Sita, if I can be careless with someone I've made, how can I expect the gods to notice me, alone in the middle of the river?

The waters were higher now, the island fast disappearing.

Something came floating out of the hut.

It was an empty kerosene tin, with one of the hens perched on top. The tin came bobbing along on the water, not far from the tree, and was then caught by the current and swept into the river. The hen still managed to keep its perch.

A little later the water must have reached the cot, because the remaining hens flew up to the rock-ledge and sat huddled there in the small recess.

The water was rising rapidly now, and all that remained of the island was the big rock that supported the hut, and the top of the hut itself, and the peepul tree.

It was a tall tree, with many branches, and it seemed unlikely that the water could ever go right over it. But how long would Sita have to remain there? She climbed a little higher, and, as she did so, a jet-black jungle crow settled in the upper branches, and Sita saw that there was a nest in them, a crow's nest, an untidy platform of twigs wedged in the fork of a branch.

In the nest were four blue-green, speckled eggs. The crow sat on them and cawed disconsolately. But though the crow was miserable, its presence brought some cheer to Sita. At least she was not alone. Better to have a crow for company than no one at all.

Other things came floating out of the hut — a large pumpkin; a red turban belonging to Grandfather, unwinding in the water like a long snake; and then — Mumta!

The doll, being filled with straw and wood-shavings, moved quite swiftly on the water and passed close to the peepul tree. Sita saw it, and wanted to call out, to urge her friend to make for the tree; but she knew that Mumta could not swim — the doll could only float, travel with the river, and perhaps be washed ashore many miles downstream.

The tree shook in the wind and the rain. The crow cawed and flew up, circled the tree a few times, and returned to the nest. Sita clung to her branch.

The tree trembled throughout its tall frame. To Sita it felt like an earthquake tremor; she felt the shudder of the tree in her own bones.

The river swirled all around her now. It was almost up to the roof of the hut. Soon the mud walls would crumble and vanish. Except for the big rock, and some trees far,

far away, there was only water to be seen.

For a moment or two Sita glimpsed a boat with several people in it moving sluggishly away from the ruins of a flooded village, and she thought she saw someone pointing towards her; but the river swept them on, and the boat was lost to view.

The river was very angry, it was like a wild beast, a dragon on the rampage, thundering down from the hills and sweeping across the plain, bringing with it dead animals, uprooted trees, household goods, and huge fish choked to death by the swirling mud.

The tall old peepul tree groaned. Its long, winding roots clung tenaciously to the earth from which the tree had sprung many, many years ago. But the earth was softening, the stones were being washed away. The roots of the tree were rapidly losing their hold.

The crow must have known that something was wrong, because it kept flying up and circling the tree, reluctant to settle in it and reluctant to fly away. As long as the nest was there, the crow would remain, flapping about and cawing in alarm.

Sita's wet cotton dress clung to her thin body. The rain ran down from her long black hair. It poured from every leaf of the tree. The crow, too, was drenched and groggy.

The tree groaned and moved again. It had seen many monsoons. Once before, it had stood firm while the river had swirled around its massive trunk. But it had been young then.

Now, old in years and tired of standing still, the tree was ready to join the river.

With a flurry of its beautiful leaves, and a surge of mud from below, the tree left its place in the earth, and, tilting, moved slowly forward, turning a little from side to side, dragging its roots along the ground. To Sita it seemed as though the river was rising to meet the sky. Then the tree moved into the main current of the river, and went a little faster, swinging Sita from side to side. Her feet were in the water but she clung tenaciously to her branch.

* * *

The branches swayed, but Sita did not lose her grip. The water was very close now. Sita was frightened. She could not see the extent of the flood or the width of the river. She could only see the immediate danger, the water surrounding the tree.

The crow kept flying around the tree. The bird was in a terrible rage. The nest was still in the branches — but not for long.... The tree lurched and twisted slightly to one side, and the nest fell into the water. Sita saw the eggs go one by one.

The crow swooped low over the water, but there was nothing it could do. In a few moments the nest had disappeared.

The bird followed the tree for about fifty yards, as though hoping that something still remained in the tree. Then, flapping its wings, it rose high into the air and flew across the river until it was out of sight.

Sita was alone once more. But there was no time for feeling lonely. Everything was in motion — up and down and sideways and forwards. "Any moment," thought Sita,

108

"the tree will turn right over and I'll be in the water!"

She saw a turtle swimming past — a great river turtle, the kind that feeds on decaying flesh. Sita turned her face away. In the distance she saw a flooded village, and people in flat-bottomed boats; but they were very far away.

Because of its great size, the tree did not move very swiftly on the river. Sometimes, when it passed into shallow water, it stopped, its roots catching in the rocks; but not for long: the river's momentum soon swept it on.

At one place, where there was a bend in the river, the tree struck a sandbank and was still.

Sita felt very tired. Her arms were aching, and she was no longer upright. With the tree almost on its side, she had to cling tightly to her branch to avoid falling off. The grey weeping sky was like a great shifting dome.

She knew she could not remain much longer in that position. It might be better to try swimming to some distant rooftop or tree. Then she heard someone calling. Craning her neck to look upriver, she was able to make out a small boat coming directly towards her.

The boat approached the tree. There was a boy in the boat who held on to one of the branches to steady himself, giving his free hand to Sita.

She grasped it, and slipped into the boat beside him.

The boy placed his bare foot against the tree-trunk and pushed away.

The little boat moved swiftly down the river. The big tree was left far behind. Sita would never see it again.

* * *

She lay stretched out in the boat, too frightened to talk. The boy looked at her, but he did not say anything, he did not even smile. He lay on his two small oars, stroking smoothly, rhythmically, trying to keep from going into the middle of the river. He wasn't strong enough to get the boat right out of the swift current; but he kept trying.

A small boat on a big river — a river that had no boundaries but which reached across the plains in all directions — the boat moved swiftly on the wild waters, and Sita's home was left far behind.

The boy wore only a loincloth. A sheathed knife was knotted into his waistband. He was a slim, wiry boy, with a hard flat belly; he had high cheekbones, strong white teeth. He was a little darker than Sita.

"You live on the island," he said at last, resting on his oars and allowing the boat to drift a little, for he had reached a broader, more placid stretch of the river. "I have seen you sometimes. But where are the others?"

"My grandmother was sick," said Sita, "so Grandfather took her to the hospital in Shahganj."

"When did they leave?"

"Early this morning."

Only that morning — and yet it seemed to Sita as though it had been many mornings ago....

"Where have you come from?" she asked. She had never seen the boy before.

"I come from — " he hesitated, "near the foothills... I was in my boat, trying to get across the river with the news that one of the villages was badly flooded, but the current was too strong. I was swept down past your island. We

110

cannot fight the river, we must go wherever it takes us."

"You must be tired. Give me the oars."

"No. There is not much to do now, except keep the boat steady."

He brought in one oar, and with his free hand he felt under the seat, where there was a small basket. He produced two mangoes, and gave one to Sita.

They bit deep into the ripe fleshy mangoes, using their teeth to tear the skin away. The sweet juice trickled down their chins. The flavour of the fruit was heavenly — truly this was the nectar of the gods! Sita hadn't tasted a mango for over a year. For a few moments she forgot about the flood — all that mattered was the mango!

The boat drifted, but not so swiftly now, for as they went further away across the plains, the river lost much of its tremendous force.

"My name is Krishan," said the boy. "My father has many cows and buffaloes, but several have been lost in the flood."

"I suppose you go to school," said Sita.

"Yes, I am supposed to go to school. There is one not far from our village. Do you have to go to school?"

"No — there is too much work at home."

It was no use wishing she was at home — home wouldn't be there any more — but she wished, at that moment, that she had another mango.

Towards evening the river changed colour. The sun, low in the sky, emerged from behind the clouds, and the river changed slowly from grey to gold, from gold to a deep orange, and then, as the sun went down, all these

111

colours were drowned in the river, and the river took on the colour of the night.

The moon was almost at the full, and Sita could see across the river, to where the trees grew on its banks.

"I will try to reach the trees," said the boy Krishan. "We do not want to spend the night on the water, do we?"

And so he pulled for the trees. After ten minutes of strenuous rowing, he reached a turn in the river and was able to escape the pull of the main current.

Soon they were in a forest, rowing between tall evergreens.

*   *   *

They moved slowly now, paddling between the trees, and the moon lighted their way, making a crooked silver path over the water.

"We will tie the boat to one of these trees," said Krishan. "Then we can rest. Tomorrow, we will have to find our way out of the forest."

He produced a length of rope from the bottom of the boat, tied one end to the boat's stern, and threw the other end over a stout branch which hung only a few feet above the water. The boat came to rest against the trunk of the tree.

It was a tall, sturdy Toon tree — the Indian Mahogany — and it was quite safe, for there was no rush of water here; and besides, the trees grew close together, making the earth firm and unyielding.

But the denizens of the forest were on the move. The animals had been flooded out of their holes, caves and

114

lairs, and were looking for shelter and dry ground.

Sita and Krishan had barely finished tying the boat to the tree when they saw a huge python gliding over the water towards them. Sita was afraid that it might try to get into the boat; but it went past them, its head above water, its great awesome length trailing behind, until it was lost in the shadows.

Krishan had more mangoes in the basket, and he and Sita sucked hungrily on them as they sat in the boat.

A big Sambur stag came threshing through the water. He did not have to swim; he was so tall that his head and shoulders remained well above the water. His antlers were big and beautiful.

"There will be other animals," said Sita. "Should we climb into the tree?"

"We are quite safe in the boat," said Krishan. "The animals are interested only in reaching dry land. They will not even hunt each other. Tonight, the deer are safe from the panther and the tiger. So lie down and sleep, and I will keep watch."

Sita stretched herself out in the boat and closed her eyes, and the sound of the water lapping against the sides of the boat soon lulled her to sleep. She woke once, when a strange bird called overhead. She raised herself on one elbow; but Krishan was awake, sitting in the prow, and he smiled reassuringly at her. He looked blue in the moonlight, the colour of the young god Krishna, and for a few moments Sita was confused and wondered if the boy was indeed Krishna; but when she thought about it, she decided that it wasn't possible, he was just a village boy and

115

she had seen hundreds like him — well, not exactly like him; he was different, in a way she couldn't explain to herself....

And when she slept again, she dreamt that the boy and Krishna were one, and she was sitting beside him on a great white bird, which flew over mountains, over the snow peaks of the Himalayas, into the cloud-land of the gods. And there was a great rumbling sound, as though the gods were angry about the whole thing, and she woke up to this terrible sound and looked about her, and there in the moonlit glade, up to his belly in water, stood a young elephant, his trunk raised as he trumpeted his predicament to the forest — for he was a young elephant, and he was lost, and he was looking for his mother.

He trumpeted again, and then lowered his head and listened. And presently, from far away, came the shrill trumpeting of another elephant. It must have been the young one's mother, because he gave several excited trumpet calls, and then went stamping and churning through the flood-water towards a gap in the trees. The boat rocked in the waves made by his passing.

"It's all right now," said Krishan. "You can go to sleep again."

"I don't think I will sleep now," said Sita.

"Then I will play my flute for you," said the boy, "and time will pass more quickly."

From the bottom of the boat he took a flute, and putting it to his lips he began to play. And the sweetest music that Sita had ever heard came pouring from the little flute, and it seemed to fill the forest with its beautiful

116

sound. And the music carried her away again, into the land of dreams, and they were riding on the bird once more, Sita and the blue god, and they were passing through clouds and mist, until suddenly the sun shot out through the clouds. And at the same moment Sita opened her eyes and saw the sun streaming through the branches of the Toon tree, its bright green leaves making a dark pattern against the blinding blue of the sky.

Sita sat up with a start, rocking the boat. There were hardly any clouds left. The trees were drenched with sunshine.

The boy Krishan was fast asleep in the bottom of the boat. His flute lay in the palm of his half-open hand. The sun came slanting across his bare brown legs. A leaf had fallen on his upturned face, but it had not woken him, it lay on his cheek as though it had grown there.

Sita did not move again. She did not want to wake the boy. It didn't look as though the water had gone down; but it hadn't risen, and that meant the flood had spent itself.

The warmth of the sun, as it crept up Krishan's body, woke him at last. He yawned, stretched his limbs, and sat up beside Sita.

"I'm hungry," he said with a smile.

"So am I," said Sita.

"The last mangoes," he said, and emptied the basket of its last two mangoes.

After they had finished the fruit, they sucked the big seeds until these were quite dry. The discarded seeds floated well on the water. Sita has always preferred them

117

to paper-boats.

"We had better move on," said Krishan.

He rowed the boat through the trees, and then for about an hour they were passing through the flooded forest, under the dripping branches of rain-washed trees. Sometimes they had to use the oars to push away vines and creepers. Sometimes drowned bushes hampered them. But they were out of the forest before noon.

Now the water was not very deep, and they were gliding over flooded fields. In the distance they saw a village. It was on high ground. In the old days, people had built their villages on hill-tops, which gave them a better defence against bandits and invading armies. This was an old village, and though its inhabitants had long ago exchanged their swords for pruning-forks, the hill on which it stood now protected it from the flood.

The people of the village — long-limbed, sturdy Jats — were generous, and gave the stranded children food and shelter. Sita was anxious to find her grandparents, and an old farmer, who had business in Shahganj, offered to take her there. She was hoping that Krishan would accompany her, but he said he would wait in the village, where he knew others would soon be arriving, his own people among them.

"You will be all right now," said Krishan. "Your grandfather will be anxious for you, so it is best that you go to him as soon as you can. And in two or three days the water will go down, and you will be able to return to the island."

"Perhaps the island has gone for ever," said Sita.

As she climbed into the farmer's bullock-cart, Krishan

120

handed her his flute.

"Please keep it for me," he said. "I will come for it one day." And, when he saw her hesitate, he added, his eyes twinkling, "It is a good flute!"

* * *

It was slow-going in the bullock-cart. The road was awash, and the wheels got stuck in the mud, and the farmer and his grown son and Sita had to keep getting down to heave and push in order to free the big wooden wheels. They were still in a foot or two of water. The bullocks were bespattered with mud, and Sita's legs were caked with it.

They were a day and a night in the bullock-cart before they reached Shahganj; and by that time, Sita, walking down the narrow bazaar of the busy market-town, was hardly recognizable.

Grandfather did not recognise her. He was walking stiffly down the road, looking straight ahead of him, and would have walked right past the dusty, dishevelled girl, if she had not charged straight at his thin, shaky legs and clasped him around the waist.

"Sita!" he cried, when he had recovered his wind and his balance. "But how are you here? How did you get off the island? I was so worried — it has been very bad these last two days...."

"Is Grandmother all right?" asked Sita.

But even as she spoke, she knew that Grandmother was no longer with them. The dazed look in the old man's eyes told her as much. She wanted to cry — not for Grandmother, who could suffer no more, but for Grandfather, who looked so helpless and bewildered; she did not want

121

him to be unhappy. She forced back her tears, and took his gnarled and trembling hand, and led him down the crowded street. And she knew, then, that it would be on her shoulder that Grandfather would have to lean in the years to come.

They returned to the island after a few days, when the river was no longer in spate. There was more rain, but the worst was over. Grandfather still had two of the goats; it had not been necessary to sell more than one.

He could hardly believe his eyes when he saw that the tree had disappeared from the island — the tree that had seemed as permanent as the island, as much a part of his life as the river itself. He marvelled at Sita's escape.

"It was the tree that saved you," he said.

"And the boy," said Sita.

Yes, and the boy.

She thought about the boy, and wondered if she would ever see him again. But she did not think too much, because there was so much to do.

For three nights they slept under a crude shelter made out of jute bags. During the day she helped Grandfather rebuild the mud hut. Once again, they used the big rock as a support.

The trunk which Sita had packed so carefully had not been swept off the island, but the water had got into it, and the food and clothing had been spoilt. But Grandfather's hookah had been saved, and, in the evenings, after their work was done and they had eaten the light meal which Sita prepared, he would smoke with a little of his old contentment, and tell Sita about other floods and storms which he had experienced as a boy.

Sita planted a mango-seed in the same spot where the peepul tree had stood. It would be many years before it grew into a big tree, but Sita liked to imagine sitting in its branches one day, picking the mangoes straight from the tree, and feasting on them all day. Grandfather was more particular about making a vegetable garden and putting down peas, carrots, gram and mustard.

One day, when most of the hard work had been done, and the new hut was almost ready, Sita took the flute which had been given to her by the boy, and walked down to the water's edge and tried to play it. But all she could produce were a few broken notes, and even the goats paid no attention to her music.

Sometimes Sita thought she saw a boat coming down the river, and she would run to meet it; but usually there was no boat, or if there was, it belonged to a stranger or to another fisherman. And so she stopped looking out for boats. Sometimes she thought she heard the music of a flute, but it seemed very distant and she could never tell where the music came from.

Slowly, the rains came to an end. The flood-waters had receded, and in the villages people were beginning to till the land again and sow crops for the winter months. There were cattle fairs and wrestling matches. The days were warm and sultry. The water in the river was no longer muddy, and one evening Grandfather brought home a huge Mahseer fish and Sita made it into a delicious curry.

*   *   *

Grandfather sat outside the hut, smoking his hookah. Sita was at the far end of the island, spreading clothes on the rocks to dry. One of the goats had followed her. It was the friendlier of the two, and often followed Sita about the island. She had made it a necklace of coloured beads.

She sat down on a smooth rock, and, as she did so, she noticed a small bright object in the sand near her feet. She stooped and picked it up. It was a little wooden toy — a coloured peacock — it must have come down on the river and been swept ashore on the island. Some of the paint had rubbed off; but for Sita, who had no toys, it was a great find. Perhaps it would speak to her, as Mumta had spoken to her.

As she held the toy peacock in the palm of her hand, she thought she heard the flute-music again; but she did not look up, she had heard it before, and she was sure that it was all in her mind.

But this time the music sounded nearer, much nearer. There was a soft footfall in the sand. And, looking up, she saw the boy, Krishan, standing over her.

"I thought you would never come," said Sita.

"I had to wait until the rains were over. Now that I am free, I will come more often. Did you keep my flute?"

"Yes, but I cannot play it properly. Sometimes it plays by itself, I think, but it will not play for me!"

"I will teach you to play it," said Krishan.

He sat down beside her, and they cooled their feet in the water, which was clear now, reflecting the blue of the sky. You could see the sand and the pebbles of the river-bed.

126

"Sometimes the river is angry, and sometimes it is kind," said Sita.

"We are part of the river," said the boy. "We cannot live without it."

It was a good river, deep and strong, beginning in the mountains and ending in the sea.

Along its banks, for hundreds of miles, lived millions of people, and Sita was only one small girl among them, and no one had ever heard of her, no one knew her — except for the old man, and the boy, and the river.

Dust on the Mountain

Winter came and went, without so much as a drizzle. The hillside was brown all summer and the fields were bare. The old plough that was dragged over the hard ground by Bisnu's lean oxen made hardly any impression. Still, Bisnu kept his seeds ready for sowing. A good monsoon, and there would be plenty of maize and rice to see the family through the next winter.

Summer went its scorching way, and a few clouds gathered on the south-western horizon.

"The monsoon is coming," announced Bisnu.

His sister Puja was at the small stream, washing clothes. "If it doesn't come soon, the stream will dry up," she said. "See, it's only a trickle this year. Remember when there were so many different flowers growing here on the banks of the stream? This year there isn't one."

"The winter was dry. It did not even snow," said Bisnu.

"I cannot remember another winter when there was no snow," said his mother. "The year your father died, there was so much snow the villagers could not light his funeral-pyre for hours.... And now there are fires everywhere." She pointed to the next mountain, half-hidden by the smoke from a forest fire.

At night they sat outside their small house, watching the fire spread. A red line stretched right across the mountain. Thousands of Himalayan trees were perishing in the flames. Oaks, deodars, maples, pines; trees that had taken hundreds of years to grow. And now a fire started carelessly by some woodcutters had been carried up the mountain with the help of the dry grass and a strong breeze. There was no one to put it out. It would take days to die down.

"If the monsoon arrives tomorrow, the fire will go out," said Bisnu, ever the optimist. He was only twelve, but he was the man in the house; he had to see that there was enough food for the family and for the oxen, for the big black dog and the hens.

There were clouds the next day but they brought only a drizzle.

"It's just the beginning," said Bisnu as he placed a bucket of muddy water on the steps.

"It usually starts with a heavy downpour," said his mother.

But there were to be no downpours that year. Clouds gathered on the horizon but they were white and puffy and soon disappeared. True monsoon clouds would have been dark and heavy with moisture. There were other signs — or lack of them — that warned of a long dry summer. The birds were silent, or simply absent. The Himalayan barbet, who usually heralded the approach of the monsoon with strident calls from the top of a spruce tree, hadn't been seen or heard. And the cicadas, who played a deafening overture in the oaks at the first hint of rain, seemed to be missing altogether.

Puja's apricot tree usually gave them a basket full of fruit every summer. This year it produced barely a handful of apricots, lacking juice and flavour. The tree looked ready to die, its leaves curled up in despair. Fortunately there was a store of walnuts, and a binful of wheat-grain and another of rice stored from the previous year, so they would not be entirely without food; but it looked as though there would be no fresh fruit or vegetables. And there would be nothing to store away for the following winter. Money would be needed to buy supplies in Tehri, some thirty miles distant. And there was no money to be earned in the village.

"I will go to Mussoorie and find work," announced Bisnu. "But Mussoorie is a two-day journey by bus," said his mother.

"There is no one there who can help you. And you may not get any work."

"In Mussoorie there is plenty of work during the summer. Rich people come up from the plains for their holidays. It is full of hotels and shops and places where they can spend their money."

"But they won't spend any money on *you*."

"There is money to be made there. And if not, I will come home. I can walk back over the Nag Tibba mountain. It will take only two and a half days and I will save the bus fare!"

"Don't go, *bhai*," pleaded Puja. "There will be no one

133

to prepare your food — you will only get sick."

But Bisnu had made up his mind so he put a few belongings in a cloth shoulder-bag, while his mother prised several rupee-coins out of a cache in the wall of their living room. Puja prepared a special breakfast of *parathas* and an egg scrambled with onions, the hen having laid just one for the occasion. Bisnu put some of the *parathas* in his bag. Then, waving goodbye to his mother and sister, he set off down the road from the village.

After walking for a mile, he reached the highway where there was a hamlet with a bus stop. A number of villagers were waiting patiently for a bus. It was an hour late but they were used to that. As long as it arrived safely and got them to their destination, they would be content. They were patient people. And although Bisnu wasn't quite so patient, he too had learnt how to wait — for late buses and late monsoons.

Along the valley and over the mountains went the little bus with its load of frail humans.

"How tiny we are," thought Bisnu, looking up at the towering peaks and the immensity of sky. "Each of us no more than a raindrop.... And I wish we had a few raindrops!"

There were still fires burning to the north but the road went south, where there were no forests anyway, just bare brown hillsides. Down near the river there were small paddy fields but unfortunately rivers ran downhill and not uphill, and there was no inexpensive way in which the water could be brought up the steep slopes to the fields that depended on rainfall.

Bisnu stared out of the bus window at the river running far below. On either bank huge boulders lay exposed, for the level of the water had fallen considerably during the past few months.

"Why are there no trees here?" he asked aloud, and received the attention of a fellow passenger, an old man in the next seat who had been keeping up a relentless dry coughing. Even though it was a warm day, he wore a woollen cap and had an old muffler wrapped about his neck.

"There were trees here once," he said, "but the contractors took the deodars for furniture and houses. And the pines were tapped to death for resin. And the oaks were stripped of their leaves to feed the cattle — you can still see a few tree-skeletons if you look hard — and the bushes that remained were finished off by the goats!"

"When did all this happen?" asked Bisnu.

"A few years ago. And it's still happening in other areas, although it's forbidden now to cut trees. The only forests that remain are in out-of-the-way places where there are no roads." A fit of coughing came over him, but he had found a good listener and was eager to continue. "The road helps you and me to get about but it also makes it easier for others to do mischief. Rich men from the cities come here and buy up what they want — land, trees, people!"

"What takes you to Mussoorie, uncle?" asked Bisnu politely. He always addressed elderly people as uncle or aunt.

"I have a cough that won't go away. Perhaps they can do something for it at the hospital in Mussoorie. Doctors

135

don't like coming to villages, you know — there's no money to be made in villages. So we must go to the doctors in the towns. I had a brother who could not be cured in Mussoorie. They told him to go to Delhi. He sold his buffaloes and went to Delhi, but there they told him it was too late to do anything. He died on the way back. I won't go to Delhi. I don't wish to die amongst strangers."

"You'll get well, uncle," said Bisnu.

"Bless you for saying so. And you — what takes you to the big town?"

"Looking for work — we need money at home."

"It is always the same. There are many like you who must go out in search of work. But don't be led astray. Don't let your friends persuade you to go to Bombay to become a film star! It is better to be hungry in your village than to be hungry on the streets of Bombay. I had a nephew who went to Bombay. The smugglers put him to work selling *afeem*— opium — and now he is in jail. Keep away from the big cities, boy. Earn your money and go home."

"I'll do that, uncle. My mother and sister will expect me to return before the summer season is over."

The old man nodded vigorously and began coughing again. Presently he dozed off. The interior of the bus smelt of tobacco smoke and petrol fumes and as a result Bisnu had a headache. He kept his face near the open window to get as much fresh air as possible, but the dust kept getting into his mouth and eyes.

Several dusty hours later the bus got into Mussoorie, honking its horn furiously at everything in sight. The

passengers, looking dazed, got down and went their different ways. The old man trudged off to the hospital.

Bisnu had to start looking for a job straightaway. He needed a lodging for the night and he could not afford the cheapest of the hotels. So he went from one shop to another, and to all the little restaurants and eating-places, asking for work — anything in exchange for a bed, a meal, and a minimum wage. A boy at one of the sweet shops told him there was a job at the Picture Palace, one of the town's three cinemas. The hill station's main road was crowded with people, for the season was just starting. Most of them were tourists who had come up from Delhi and other large towns.

The street lights had come on, and the shops were lighting up, when Bisnu presented himself at the Picture Palace.

The man who ran the cinema's tea-stall had just sacked the previous helper for his general clumsiness. Whenever he engaged a new boy (which was fairly often) he started him off with the warning:

"I will be keeping a record of all the cups and plates you break, and their cost will be deducted from your salary at the end of the month."

As Bisnu's salary had been fixed at fifty rupees a month, he would have to be very careful if he was going to receive any of it.

"In my first month," said Chittru, one of the three tea-stall boys, "I broke six cups and five saucers, and my pay came to three rupees! Better be careful!"

Bisnu's job was to help prepare the tea and samosas,

138

serve these refreshments to the public during intervals in the film, and later wash up the dishes. In addition to his salary, he was allowed to drink as much tea as he wanted or could hold in his stomach.

Bisnu went to work immediately and it was not long before he was as well-versed in his duties as the other two tea-boys, Chittru and Bali. Chittru was an easy-going, lazy boy who always tried to place the brunt of his work on someone else's shoulders. But he was generous and lent Bisnu five rupees during the first week. Bali, besides being a tea-boy, had the enviable job of being the poster-boy. As the cinema was closed during the mornings, Bali would be busy either in pushing the big poster-board around Mussoorie, or sticking posters on convenient walls.

"Posters are very useful," he claimed. "They prevent old walls from falling down."

Chittru had relatives in Mussoorie and slept at their house. But both Bisnu and Bali were on their own and had to sleep at the cinema. After the last show the hall was locked up, so they could not settle down in the expensive seats as they would have liked! They had to sleep in the foyer, near the ticket-office, where they were often at the mercy of icy Himalayan winds.

Bali made things more comfortable by setting his poster-board at an angle to the wall, which gave them a little alcove where they could sleep protected from the wind. As they had only one blanket each, they placed their blankets together and rolled themselves into a tight warm ball.

During shows, when Bisnu took the tea around, there was nearly always someone who would be rude and offensive. Once when he spilt some tea on a college student's shoes, he received a hard kick on the shin. He complained to the tea-stall owner, but his employer said, "The customer is always right. You should have got out of the way in time!"

As he began to get used to this life, Bisnu found himself taking an interest in some of the regular customers.

There was, for instance, the large gentleman with the soup-strainer moustache, who drank his tea from the saucer. As he drank, his lips worked like a suction pump, and the tea, after a brief agitation in the saucer, would disappear in a matter of seconds. Bisnu often wondered if there was something lurking in the forests of that gentleman's upper lip, something that would suddenly spring out and fall upon him! The boys took great pleasure in exchanging anecdotes about the peculiarities of some of the customers.

Bisnu had never seen such bright, painted women before. The girls in his village, including his sister Puja, were good-looking and often sturdy; but they did not use perfumes or make-up like these more prosperous women from the towns of the plains. Wearing expensive clothes and jewellery, they never gave Bisnu more than a brief, bored glance. Other women were more inclined to notice him, favouring him with kind words and a small tip when he took away the cups and plates. He found he could make a few rupees a month in tips; and when he received his first month's pay, he was able to send most of it home.

Chittru accompanied him to the post office and helped him to fill in the money-order form. Bisnu had been to the village school, but he wasn't used to forms and official paper-work. Chittru, a town boy, knew all about them, even though he could just read and write.

Walking back to the cinema, Chittru said, '"We can make more money at the limestone quarries."

"All right, let's try it," said Bisnu.

"Not now," said Chittru, who enjoyed the busy season in the hill station. "After the season — after the monsoon."

But there was still no monsoon to speak of, just an occasional drizzle which did little to clear the air of the dust that blew up from the plains. Bisnu wondered how his mother and sister were faring at home. A wave of homesickness swept over him. The hill station, with all its glitter, was just a pretty gift box with nothing inside.

One day in the cinema Bisnu saw the old man who had been with him on the bus. He greeted him like a long lost friend. At first the old man did not recognise the boy, but when Bisnu asked him if he had recovered from his illness, the old man remembered and said, "So you are still in Mussoorie, boy. That is good. I thought you might have gone down to Delhi to make more money." He added that he was a little better and that he was undergoing a course of treatment at the hospital. Bisnu brought him a cup of tea and refused to take any money for it; it could be included in his own quota of free tea. When the show was over, the old man went his way and Bisnu did not see him again.

In September the town began to empty. The taps were running dry or giving out just a trickle of muddy water. A thick mist lay over the mountain for days on end, but there was no rain. When the mists cleared, an autumn wind came whispering through the deodars.

At the end of the month the manager of the Picture Palace gave everyone a week's notice, a week's pay, and announced that the cinema would be closing for the winter.

Bali said, "I'm going to Delhi to find work. I'll come back next summer. What about you, Bisnu, why don't you come with me? It's easier to find work in Delhi."

"I'm staying with Chittru," said Bisnu. "We may work at the quarries."

"I like the big towns," said Bali. "I like shops and people and lots of noise. I will never go back to my village. There is no money there, no fun."

Bali made a bundle of his things and set out for the bus stand. Chittru bought himself a pair of cheap shoes, for the old ones had fallen to pieces. With what was left of his money, he sent another money-order home. Then he and Chittru set out for the limestone quarries, an eight-mile walk from Mussoorie.

They knew they were nearing the quarries when they saw clouds of limestone dust hanging in the air. The dust hid the next mountain from view. When they did see the mountain, they found that the top of it was missing — blasted away by dynamite to enable the quarriers to get at the rich strata of limestone rock below the surface.

142

The skeletons of a few trees remained on the lower slopes. Almost everything else had gone — grass, flowers, shrubs, birds, butterflies, grasshoppers, ladybirds.... A rock lizard popped its head out of a crevice to look at the intruders. Then, like some prehistoric survivor, it scuttled back into its underground shelter.

"I used to come here when I was small," announced Chittru cheerfully.

"Were the quarries here then?"

"Oh, no. My friends and I — we used to come for the strawberries. They grew all over this mountain. Wild strawberries, but very tasty."

"Where are they now?" asked Bisnu, looking around at the devastated hillside.

"All gone," said Chittru. "Maybe there are some on the next mountain."

Even as they approached the quarries, a blast shook the hillside. Chittru pulled Bisnu under an overhanging rock to avoid the shower of stones that pelted down on the road. As the dust enveloped them, Bisnu had a fit of coughing. When the air cleared a little, they saw the limestone dump ahead of them.

Chittru, who was older and bigger than Bisnu, was immediately taken on as a labourer; but the quarry foreman took one look at Bisnu and said. "You're too small. You won't be able to break stones or lift those heavy rocks and load them into the trucks. Be off, boy. Find something else to do."

He was offered a job in the labourers' canteen, but he'd had enough of making tea and washing dishes. He

143

was about to turn round and walk back to Mussoorie when he felt a heavy hand descend on his shoulder. He looked up to find a grey-bearded turbaned Sikh looking down at him in some amusement.

"I need a cleaner for my truck," he said. "The work is easy, but the hours are long!"

Bisnu responded immediately to the man's gruff but jovial manner.

"What will you pay?" he asked.

"Fifteen rupees a day, and you'll get food and a bed at the depot."

"As long as I don't have to cook the food," said Bisnu.

The truck driver laughed. "You might prefer to do so, once you've tasted the depot food. Are you coming on my truck? Make up your mind."

"I'm your man," said Bisnu; and waving goodbye to Chittru, he followed the Sikh to his truck.

A horn blared, shattering the silence of the mountains, and the truck came round the bend in the road. A herd of goats scattered to left and right.

The goatherds cursed as a cloud of dust enveloped them, and then the truck had left them behind and was rattling along the bumpy, unmetalled road to the quarries.

At the wheel of the truck, stroking his grey moustache with one hand, sat Pritam Singh. It was his own truck. He had never allowed anyone else to drive it. Every day he made two trips to the quarries, carrying truckloads of limestone back to the depot at the bottom of the hill. He was paid by the trip and he was always anxious to get in

144

two trips every day.

Sitting beside him was Bisnu, his new cleaner. In less than a month Bisnu had become an experienced hand at looking after trucks, riding in them, and even sleeping in them. He got on well with Pritam, the grizzled, fifty-year-old Sikh, who boasted of his two well-off sons — one a farmer in the Punjab, the other a wine merchant in far-off London. He could have gone to live with either of them, but his sturdy independence kept him on the road in his battered old truck.

Pritam pressed hard on his horn. Now there was no one on the road — neither beast nor man — but Pritam was fond of the sound of his horn and liked blowing it. He boasted that it was the loudest horn in northern India. Although it struck terror into the hearts of all who heard it — for it was louder than the trumpeting of an elephant — it was music to Pritam's ears.

Pritam treated Bisnu as an equal and a friendly banter had grown between them during their many trips together.

"One more year on this bone-breaking road," said Pritam, "and then I'll sell my truck and retire."

"But who will buy such a shaky old truck," said Bisnu. "It will retire before you do!"

"Now don't be insulting, boy. She's only twenty years old — there are still a few years left in her!" And as though to prove it, he blew the horn again. Its strident sound echoed and re-echoed down the mountain gorge. A pair of wildfowl burst from the bushes and fled to more silent regions.

Pritam's thoughts went to his dinner.

"Haven't had a good meal for days."

"Haven't had a good meal for *weeks*," said Bisnu, although in fact he looked much healthier than when he had worked at the cinema's tea-stall.

"Tonight I'll give you a dinner in a good hotel. Tandoori chicken and rice pullao," Pritam said. He sounded his horn again as though to put a seal on his promise. Then he slowed down, because the road had become narrow and precipitous, and trotting ahead of them was a train of mules.

As the horn blared, one mule ran forward, another ran backward. One went uphill, another went downhill. Soon there were mules all over the place. Pritam cursed the mules and the mule-drivers cursed Pritam; but he had soon left them far behind.

Along this range, all the hills were bare and dry. Most of the forest had long since disappeared.

"Are your hills as bare as these?" asked Pritam.

"No, we still have some trees," said Bisnu, "Nobody has started blasting the hills as yet. In front of our house there is a walnut tree which gives us two baskets of walnuts every year. And there is an apricot tree. But it was a bad year for fruit. There was no rain. And the stream is too far away."

"It will rain soon," said Pritam. "I can smell rain. It is coming from the north. The winter will be early."

"It will settle the dust."

Dust was everywhere. The truck was full of it. The leaves of the shrubs and the few trees were thick with it. Bisnu

148

could feel the dust under his eyelids and in his mouth. And as they approached the quarries, the dust increased. But it was a different kind of dust now — whiter, stinging the eyes, irritating the nostrils.

They had been blasting all morning.

"Let's wait here," said Pritam, bringing the truck to a halt.

They sat in silence, staring through the windscreen at the scarred cliffs a little distance down the road. There was a sharp crack of explosives and the hillside blossomed outwards. Earth and rocks hurtled down the mountain.

Bisnu watched in awe as shrubs and small trees were flung into the air. It always frightened him — not so much the sight of the rocks bursting asunder, as the trees being flung aside and destroyed. He thought of the trees at home — the walnut, the chestnuts, the pines — and wondered if one day they would suffer the same fate, and whether the mountains would all become a desert like this particular range. No trees, no grass, no water — only the choking dust of mines and quarries.

Pritam pressed hard on his horn again, to let the people at the site know that he was approaching. He parked outside a small shed where the contractor and the foreman were sipping cups of tea. A short distance away, some labourers, Chittru among them, were hammering at chunks of rock, breaking them up into manageable pieces. A pile of stones stood ready for loading, while the rock that had just been blasted lay scattered about the hillside.

"Come and have a cup of tea," called out the contractor.

"I can't hang about all day," said Pritam. "There's another trip to make — and the days are getting shorter. I don't want to be driving by night."

But he sat down on a bench and ordered two cups of tea from the stall. The foreman strolled over to the group of labourers and told them to start loading. Bisnu let down the grid at the back of the truck. Then, to keep himself warm, he began helping Chittru and the men with the loading.

"Don't expect to be paid for helping," said the contractor, for whom every rupee spent was a rupee off his profits.

"Don't worry," said Bisnu. "I don't work for contractors, I work for friends."

"That's right," called out Pritam. "Mind what you say to Bisnu — he's no one's servant!"

The contractor wasn't happy until there was no space left for a single stone. Then Bisnu had his cup of tea and three of the men climbed on the pile of stones in the open truck.

"All right, let's go!" said Pritam. "I want to finish early today — Bisnu and I are having a big dinner!"

Bisnu jumped in beside Pritam, banging the door shut. It never closed properly unless it was slammed really hard. But it opened at a touch.

"This truck is held together with sticking plaster," joked Pritam. He was in good spirits. He started the engine, and blew his horn just as he passed the foreman and the contractor.

"They are deaf in one ear from the blasting," said Pritam. "I'll make them deaf in the other ear!"

The labourers were singing as the truck swung round the sharp bends of the winding road. The door beside Bisnu rattled on its hinges. He was feeling quite dizzy.

"Not too fast," he said.

"Oh," said Pritam. "And since when did you become nervous about my driving?"

"It's just today," said Bisnu uneasily. "It's a feeling, that's all."

"You're getting old," said Pritam. "That's your trouble."

"I suppose so," said Bisnu.

Pritam was feeling young. He drove faster.

As they swung round a bend, Bisnu looked out of his window. All he saw was the sky above and the valley below. They were very near the edge; but here it was usually like that on this narrow mountain road.

After a few more hairpin bends, the road descended steeply to the valley. Just then a stray mule ran into the middle of the road. Pritam swung the steering wheel over to the right to avoid the mule. The road turned sharply to the left, and the truck went over the edge.

As it tipped over, hanging for a few seconds on the edge of the cliff, the labourers leapt from the back of the truck. It pitched forward, and as it struck a rock outcrop, the loose door burst open. Bisnu was thrown out.

The truck hurtled forward, bouncing over the rocks, turning over on its side and rolling over twice before

151

coming to rest against the trunk of a scraggy old oak tree. But for the tree, the truck would have plunged several hundred feet down to the bottom of the gorge.

The labourers sat on the hillside, stunned and badly shaken. The other man had picked himself up and was running back to the quarry for help.

Bisnu had landed in a bed of nettles. He was smarting all over, but he wasn't really hurt.

His first impulse was to get up and run back to the road. Then he realised that Pritam was still in the truck.

Bisnu skidded down the steep slope, calling out, "Pritam uncle, are you all right?"

There was no answer.

When Bisnu saw Pritam's arm and half his body jutting out of the open door of the truck, he feared the worst. It was a strange position, half in and half out. Bisnu was about to turn away and climb back up the hill, when he noticed that Pritam had opened a blackened and swollen eye. It looked straight up at Bisnu.

"Are you alive?" whispered Bisnu, terrified.

"What do you think?" muttered Pritam. He closed his eye again.

When the contractor and his men arrived, it took them almost an hour to get Pritam Singh out of the wreckage of the truck, and another hour to get him to the hospital in the next big town. He had broken bones and fractured ribs and a dislocated shoulder. But the doctors said he was repairable — which was more than could be said for the truck.

"So the truck's finished," said Pritam, when Bisnu

came to see him after a couple of days. "Now I'll have to go home and live with my son. And what about you, boy? I can get you a job on a friend's truck."

"No," said Bisnu, "I'll be going home soon."

"And what will you do at home?"

"I'll work on my land. It's better to grow things on the land than to blast things out of it."

They were silent for some time.

"There is something to be said for growing things," said Pritam. "But for that tree, the truck would have finished up at the foot of the mountain, and I wouldn't be here, all bandaged up and talking to you. It was the tree that saved me. Remember that, boy."

"I'll remember. And I won't forget the dinner you promised me, either."

It snowed during Bisnu's last night at the quarries. He slept near Chittru, in a large shed meant for the labourers. The wind blew the snow-flakes in at the entrance; it whistled down the deserted mountain pass. In the morning Bisnu opened his eyes to a world of dazzling whiteness. The snow was piled high against the walls of the shed, and they had some difficulty getting out.

Bisnu joined Chittru at the tea-stall, drank a glass of hot sweet tea, and ate two buns. He said goodbye to Chittru and set out on the long march home. The road would be closed to traffic because of the heavy snow, and he would have to walk all the way.

He trudged over the hills all day, stopping only at small villages to take refreshment. By nightfall he was still ten miles from home. But he had fallen in with other travel-

153

lers, and with them he took shelter at an inn. They built a fire and crowded round it, and each man spoke of his home and fields and all were of the opinion that the snow and rain had come just in time to save the winter crops. Someone sang, and another told a ghost story. Feeling at home already, Bisnu fell asleep listening to their tales. In the morning they parted and went different ways.

It was almost noon when Bisnu reached his village.

The fields were covered with snow and the mountain stream was in spate. As he climbed the terraced fields to his house, he heard the sound of barking, and his mother's big black mastiff came bounding towards him over the snow. The dog jumped on him and licked his arms and then went bounding back to the house to tell the others.

Puja saw him from the courtyard and ran indoors shouting, "Bisnu has come, my brother has come!"

His mother ran out of the house, calling "Bisnu, Bisnu!"

Bisnu came walking through the fields, and he did not hurry, he did not run; he wanted to savour the moment of his return, with his mother and sister smiling, waiting for him in front of the house. There was no need to hurry now. He would be with them for a long time, and the manager of the Picture Palace would have to find someone else for the summer season... It was his home, and these were his fields! Even the snow was his. When the snow melted he would clear the fields, and nourish them, and make them rich.

He felt very big and very strong as he came striding over the land he loved.

154

Grandfather's Private Zoo

The Adventures of Toto

Grandfather bought Toto from a tonga-driver for the sum of five rupees. The tonga-driver used to keep the little red monkey tied to a feeding-trough, and the monkey looked so out of place there that Grandfather decided he would add the little fellow to his private zoo.

Toto was a pretty monkey. His bright eyes sparkled with mischief beneath deep-set eyebrows, and his teeth, which were a pearly white, were very often displayed in a smile that frightened the life out of elderly Anglo-Indian ladies. But his hands looked dried-up as though they had been pickled in the sun for many years. Yet his fingers were quick and wicked; and his tail, while adding to his good looks (Grandfather believed a tail would add to anyone's good looks), also served as a third hand. He could use it to hang from a branch; and it was capable of scooping up any delicacy that might be out of reach of his hands.

Grandmother always fussed when Grandfather brought home some new bird or animal. So it was decided that Toto's presence should be kept a secret from her until she was in a particularly good mood. Grandfather and I put him away in a little closet opening into my bedroom wall, where he was tied securely — or so we thought — to a peg fastened into the wall.

A few hours later, when Grandfather and I came back to release Toto, we found that the walls, which had been covered with some ornamental paper chosen by Grandfather, now stood out as naked brick and plaster. The peg in the wall had been wrenched from its socket, and my school blazer, which had been hanging there, was in shreds. I wondered what Grandmother would say. But Grandfather didn't worry; he seemed pleased with Toto's performance.

"He's clever," said Grandfather. "Given time, I'm sure he could have tied the torn pieces of your blazer into a rope, and made his escape from the window!"

His presence in the house still a secret, Toto was now transferred to a big cage in the servants' quarters where a number of Grandfather's pets lived very sociably together — a tortoise, a pair of rabbits, a tame squirrel and, for a while, my pet goat. But the monkey wouldn't allow any of his companions to sleep at night; so Grandfather, who had to leave Dehra Dun next day to collect his pension in Saharanpur, decided to take him along.

Unfortunately I could not accompany Grandfather on that trip, but he told me about it afterwards. A big black canvas kit-bag was provided for Toto. This, with some straw at the bottom, became his new abode. When the strings of the bag were tied, there was no escape. Toto could not get his hands through the opening, and the

158

canvas was too strong for him to bite his way through. His efforts to get out only had the effect of making the bag roll about on the floor or occasionally jump into the air — an exhibition that attracted a curious crowd of onlookers on the Dehra Dun railway platform.

Toto remained in the bag as far as Saharanpur, but while Grandfather was producing his ticket at the railway-turnstile, Toto suddenly poked his head out of the bag and gave the ticket-collector a wide grin.

The poor man was taken aback; but, with great presence of mind and much to Grandfather's annoyance, he said, "Sir, you have a dog with you. You'll have to pay for it accordingly."

In vain did Grandfather take Toto out of the bag; in vain did he try to prove that a monkey did not qualify as a dog, or even as a quadruped. Toto was classified a dog by the ticket-collector; and three rupees was the sum handed over as his fare.

Then Grandfather, just to get his own back, took from his pocket our pet tortoise, and said, "What must I pay for this, since you charge for all animals?"

The ticket-collector looked closely at the tortoise, prodded it with his forefinger, gave Grandfather a pleased and triumphant look, and said, "No charge. It is not a dog."

When Toto was finally accepted by Grandmother he was given a comfortable home in the stable, where he had for a companion the family donkey, Nana. On Toto's first night in the stable, Grandfather paid him a visit to see if he was comfortable. To his surprise he found Nana, without apparent cause, pulling at her halter and trying to keep her head as far as possible from a bundle of hay.

Grandfather gave Nana a slap across her haunches, and she jerked back, dragging Toto with her. He had fastened on to her long ears with his sharp little teeth.

Toto and Nana never became friends.

A great treat for Toto during cold winter evenings was the large bowl of warm water given him by Grandmother for his bath. He would cunningly test the temperature with his hand, then gradually step into the bath, first one foot, then the other (as he had seen me doing), until he was in the water up to his neck. Once comfortable, he would take the soap in his hands or feet, and rub himself all over. When the water became cold, he would get out and run as quickly as he could to the kitchen-fire in order to dry himself. If anyone laughed at him during this performance, Toto's feelings would be hurt and he would refuse to go on with his bath.

One day Toto nearly succeeded in boiling himself alive.

A large kitchen kettle had been left on the fire to boil for tea. And Toto, finding himself with nothing better to do, decided to remove the lid. Finding the water just warm enough for a bath, he got in, with his head sticking out from the open kettle. This was just fine for a while, until the water began to boil. Toto then raised himself a little; but, finding it cold outside, sat down again. He continued hopping up and down for some time, until Grandmother arrived and hauled him, half-boiled, out of the kettle.

If there is a part of the brain especially devoted to mischief, that part was largely developed in Toto. He was always tearing things to pieces. Whenever one of my aunts came near him, he made every effort to get hold of her dress and tear a hole in it.

One day, at lunch-time, a large dish of pullao-rice stood in the centre of the dining-table. We entered the room to find Toto stuffing himself with rice. My grandmother screamed — and Toto threw a plate at her. One of my aunts rushed forward — and received a glass of water in the face. When Grandfather arrived, Toto picked up the dish of pullao and made his exit through a window. We found him in the branches of the jackfruit tree, the dish still in his arms. He remained there all afternoon, eating slowly through the rice, determined on finishing every grain. And then, in order to spite Grandmother, who had screamed at him, he threw the dish down from the tree, and chattered with delight when it broke into a hundred pieces.

Obviously Toto was not the sort of pet we could keep for long. Even Grandfather realised that. We were not well-to-do, and could not afford the frequent loss of dishes, clothes, curtains and wallpaper. So Grandfather found the tonga-driver, and sold Toto back to him — for only three rupees.

The Conceited Python

There was one pet which Grandfather could not keep for very long. Grandmother was tolerant of some birds and animals, but she drew the line at reptiles. Even a chameleon as sweet-tempered as Henry (we will come to him later) made her blood run cold. Grandfather should have known that there was little chance of being allowed to keep a python.

He never could resist buying unusual pets, and while we still had Toto, he paid a snake-charmer in the bazar only four rupees for the young four-foot python that was on display to a crowd of eager boys and girls. Grandfather impressed the gathering by slinging the python over his shoulders and walking home with it.

The first to see them arrive was Toto, swinging from a branch of the jack-fruit tree. One look at the python, ancient enemy of his race, and he fled into the house, squealing with fright. The noise brought Grandmother on to the verandah, where she nearly fainted at the sight of the python curled round Grandfather's throat.

"It will strangle you to death," she cried. "Get rid of it

at once!"

"Nonsense!" said Grandfather. "He's only a young fellow — he'll soon get used to us."

"He might, indeed," said Grandmother, "but I have no intention of getting used to him. And you know your cousin Mabel is coming to stay with us tomorrow. She'll leave the minute she knows there's a snake in the house."

"Well, perhaps we should show it to her as soon as she arrives," said Grandfather, who did not look forward to the visits of relatives any more than I did.

"You'll do no such thing," said Grandmother.

"Well, I can't let it loose in the garden. It might find its way into the poultry house, and then where would we be?"

"Oh, how irritating you are!" grumbled Grandmother. "Lock the thing in the bathroom, then go out and find the man you bought it from, and get him to come here and collect it."

And so, in my awestruck presence, Grandfather took the python into the bathroom and placed it in the tub. After closing the door on it, be gave me a sad look.

"Perhaps Grandmother is right this time," he said. "After all, we don't want the snake to get hold of Toto. And it's sure to be very hungry."

He hurried off to the bazar to look for the snake-charmer, and was gone for about two hours, while Grandmother paced up and down the verandah. When Grandfather returned, looking crestfallen, we knew he had not been able to find the snake-charmer.

"Well, then, kindly take it away yourself," said Grandmother. "Leave it in the jungle across the river-bed."

"All right, but let me feed it first," said Grandfather. He produced a plucked chicken (in those days you could get a chicken for less than a rupee), and went into the bathroom, followed, in single file, by myself, Grandmother, and the cook and gardener.

Grandfather opened the door and stepped into the room. I peeped round his legs, while the others stayed well behind. We could not see the python anywhere.

"He's gone," announced Grandfather.

"He couldn't have gone far," said Grandmother. "Look *under* the tub."

We looked under the tub, but the python was not there. Then Grandfather went to the window. "We left it open," he said. "He must have gone this way."

A careful search was made of the house, the kitchen, the garden, the stable and the poultry shed; but the python could not be found anywhere.

"He must have gone over the garden wall," said Grandfather. "He'll be well away by now."

"I certainly hope so," said Grandmother, with a look of relief.

Aunt Mabel arrived the next day for a three-week visit, and for a couple of days Grandfather and I were a little worried in case the python made a sudden appearance; but on the third day, when he did not show up, we felt sure that he had gone for good.

And then, towards evening, we were startled by a scream from the garden. Seconds later Aunt Mabel came flying up the verandah steps, looking as though she had seen the devil himself.

"In the guava tree!" she gasped. "I was reaching for a guava when I saw it staring at me. The *look* in its eyes! As though it would eat me alive..."

"Calm down, my dear," urged Grandmother, sprinkling eau-de-cologne over my aunt. "Tell us, what *did* you see?"

"A snake!" sobbed Aunt Mabel. "A great boa-constrictor. It must have been twenty feet long! In the guava tree. Its eyes were terrible. And it looked at me in such a *queer* way...."

My grandparents exchanged glances, and Grandfather said: "I'll go out and kill it." Taking hold of an umbrella, he sallied forth into the garden. But when he got to the guava tree, the python had gone.

"Aunt Mabel must have frightened it away," I said.

"Hush," said Grandfather. "We mustn't speak of your aunt in that way." But his eyes were alive with laughter.

After this incident, the python began to make a number of appearances, always in the most unexpected places. Aunt Mabel had another fit when she saw him emerge from beneath a cushion. She packed her bags and left.

The hunt continued.

One morning I saw the python curled up on the dressing-table, gazing at his own reflection in the mirror. I went for Grandfather, but by the time we returned to the room the python had moved on. He was seen in the garden, and once the cook saw him crawling up the iron ladder to the roof. Then we found him on the dressing-table a second time, admiring himself in the mirror. Evidently he was fascinated by his own reflection.

"All the attention he's getting has probably made him conceited," said Grandfather.

"He's trying to look better for Aunt Mabel," I said. (I regretted this remark because Grandmother overheard and held up my pocket money for the rest of the week.)

"Anyway, now we know his weakness," said Grandfather.

"Are *you* trying to be funny too?" said Grandmother.

"I didn't mean Aunt Mabel," explained Grandfather. "The python is becoming vain, so it should be easier to catch him."

Grandfather set about preparing a large cage, with a mirror at one end. In the cage he left a juicy chicken and several other tasty things. The opening was fitted up with a trap-door.

Aunt Mabel had already left by the time we set up the trap, but we had to go on with the project because we could not have the python prowling about the house indefinitely. A python's bite is not poisonous, but it can swallow a live monkey, and it can be a risky playmate for a small boy.

For a few days nothing happened; and then, as I was leaving for school one morning, I saw the python in the cage. He had eaten everything left out for him, and was curled up in front of the mirror, with something that resembled a smile on his face — if you can imagine a python smiling.

I lowered the trap-door gently, but the python took no

167

notice of me. Grandfather and the gardener put the cage in a tonga and took it across the river-bed. Opening the trap-door, they left the cage in the jungle. When they went away, the python had made no attempt to get out.

"I didn't have the heart to take the mirror away from him," said Grandfather. "It's the first time I've seen a snake fall in love."

A Hornbill Called Harold

Harold's mother, like all good hornbills, was the most careful of wives; his father, the most easy-going of husbands. In January before the dhak tree burst into flame-red blossom, Harold's father took his wife into a great hole high in the tree trunk, where his father and his father's father had taken their brides at the same time every year. In this weather-beaten hollow, generation upon generation of hornbills had been raised; and Harold's mother, like those before her, was enclosed within the hole by a sturdy wall of earth, sticks and dung.

Harold's father left a small slit in the centre of this wall, to enable him to communicate with his wife whenever he felt like a chat. Walled up in her uncomfortable room, Harold's mother was a prisoner for over two months. During this period an egg was laid, and Harold was born.

In his naked boyhood Harold was no beauty. His most prominent feature was his flaming red bill, matching the blossoms of the flame-tree which were now ablaze, heralding the summer. He had a stomach that could never be filled, despite the best efforts of his parents, who

169

brought him pieces of jackfruit and berries from the banyan tree.

As he grew bigger, the room became more cramped, and one day his mother burst through the wall, spread out her wings and sailed over the tree-tops. Her husband pretended he was glad to see her about, and played with her, expressing his delight with deep gurgles and throaty chuckles. Then they repaired the wall of the nursery, so that Harold would not fall out.

Harold was quite happy in his cell, and felt no urge for freedom. He was putting on weight and feathers, and acquiring a philosophy of his own. Then something happened to change the course of his life.

One afternoon he was awakened from his siesta by a loud banging on the wall, a banging quite different from that made by his parents. Soon the wall gave way, and there was something large and red staring at him — not his parents' bills, but Grandfather's sun-burnt face and short red beard.

In a moment Harold was seized. He roared lustily and struck out with his bill and feet, but to no purpose. Grandfather had him in a bag, and the young hornbill was added to the zoo on our front verandah.

Harold had a simple outlook, and once he had got over some early attacks of nerves, he began to welcome the approach of strangers. For him, Grandfather and I meant the arrival of food, and he greeted us with craning neck, quivering open bill, and a loud, croaking *"Ka-Ka-Kaee!"* Grandfather gave him a very roomy cage in a sunny corner of the verandah — a palace compared to the

170

cramped quarters he had grown up in — and a basin of fresh water every day for his bath.

Harold was not beautiful by Indian standards. He had a small body and a large head. But his nature was friendly, and he stayed on good terms with both my grandparents during his twelve years as a member of the household. He would even tolerate my aunts, to whom most of the other pets in the house usually took a strong dislike.

Harold's best friends were those who fed him, and he was willing even to share his food with us, sometimes trying to feed me with his great beak. Eating was a serious business for Harold, and if there was any delay at meal-times he would summon us with raucous barks and vigorous bangs of his bill on the woodwork of his cage.

He loved bananas and dates and balls of boiled rice. I would throw him the rice-balls, and he would catch them in his beak, toss them into the air, and let them drop into his open mouth. He perfected his trick of catching things, and Grandfather trained him to catch a tennis ball thrown with some force from a distance of fifteen yards. Harold would have made an excellent slip-fielder at cricket.

Having no family, profession or religion, Harold gave much time and thought to his personal appearance. He carried a rouge-pot on his person, and used it very skilfully as an item of his morning toilet. This rouge-pot was a small gland situated above the roots of his tail feathers; it produced a rich yellow fluid. Harold would dip into his rouge-pot from time to time and then rub the colour over his feathers and the back of his neck. The colour came

171

off on one's hands when one touched Harold. I think his colour had some sort of waterproofing effect because he used his colour-pot most during the rains.

Harold never drank anything, not even water, in all the years he stayed with Grandfather. Apparently hornbills get all the liquid they need from their solid food.

Only once did he misbehave. That was when he removed a lighted cigar from the hand of an American friend who was visiting us, and swallowed it. It was a moving experience for Harold, and an unnerving one for our guest. Both had to be given some brandy.

Though Harold drank no water, he loved the rain. We always knew when it was going to rain, because Harold would start chuckling to himself about one hour before the raindrops fell. This used to irritate my aunts. They were always being caught in the rain. Harold would be chuckling when they left the house; and when they returned drenched to the skin, he would be in fits of laughter.

As the storm-clouds gathered, and gusts of wind shook the banana trees, Harold would get very excited, and his chuckle would change to an eerie whistle. *"Wheee...wheee"* he would scream. And then, as the first drops of rain hit the verandah steps, and the scent of the freshened earth passed through the house, he would start roaring again, like a drunk. The wind swept the rain into his spacious cage, and Harold would spread out his wings and dance, tumbling about like a circus clown.

When the monsoon really set in, he would get used to the rains, and his enthusiasm, like our own, would lessen.

But the first few showers were always a wonder to him and we would come out on the verandah to watch him and share in his pleasure.

I miss Harold's raucous bark, and the banging of his great bill. If there is a heaven for good hornbills, I hope he is getting all the summer showers he could wish for, and plenty of tennis balls to catch.

A Little World of Mud

I had never thought there was much to be found in the rain-water pond behind our house except for quantities of mud and the occasional water-buffalo. It was Grandfather who introduced me to the pond's diversity of life, so beautifully arranged that each individual gained some benefit from the well-being of the mass. To the inhabitants of the pond, the pond was the world; and to the inhabitants of the world, commented Grandfather, the world was but a muddy pond.

When Grandfather first showed me the pond-world, he chose a dry place in the shade of an old peepul tree, where we sat for an hour, gazing steadily at the thin green scum on the water. The buffaloes had not arrived for their afternoon dip, and the surface of the pond was undisturbed.

For the first ten minutes we saw nothing. Then a small black blob appeared in the middle of the pond. Gradually it rose higher until at last we could make out a frog's head, its big eyes staring hard at us. He did not know if we were friend or enemy, and kept his body out of sight.

A heron, his mortal enemy, might have been wading about in search of him. When he had made sure that we were not herons, he passed this information on to his friends and neighbours, and very soon there were a number of big heads and eyes on the surface of the water. Throats swelled, and there began a chorus which went, *"wurk, wurk, wurk..."*

In the shallow water near the tree we could see a dark shifting shadow. When we touched it with the end of a stick, the dark mass immediately became alive. Thousands of little black tadpoles wriggled into life, pushing and hustling one another.

"What do tadpoles eat?" I asked Grandfather.

"They eat one another much of the time," said Grandfather, who had once kept a few in an aquarium. "It may seem an unpleasant custom, but when you think of the thousands of tadpoles that are hatched, you will realise what a useful system it is. If all the young tadpoles in this pond became frogs, they would take up every inch of ground between us and the house!"

"Their croaking would certainly drive Grandmother crazy," I said, to which Grandfather agreed.

When Grandfather was younger, he had once brought home a number of green tree-frogs. He put them in a glass-jar and left them on a window-sill without telling anyone, anyone at all, of their presence.

At about four in the morning the entire household was awakened by a loud and fearful noise, and Grandmother and several nervous relatives gathered on the verandah for safety. Their fear turned to anger when they discov-

175

ered the source of the noise. At the first glimmer of dawn, the frogs had with one accord burst into song. Grandmother wanted to throw the frogs, bottle and all, out of the window, but Grandfather gave the bottle a good shaking, and the frogs stayed quiet. Everyone went to sleep again, but Grandfather was obliged to stay awake in order to shake the bottle whenever the frogs showed signs of bursting into song again.

Fortunately for all concerned, the next day Aunt Mabel took the top off the bottle to see what was inside. The sight of a dozen green tree-frogs so frightened her that she ran off without replacing the cover, and the frogs jumped out and got loose in the garden and were never seen again.

Their escape ruined Grandfather's project of using the tree-frogs as barometers. His idea was to place the frogs in tall bottles with wooden ladders. The steps of the ladder would act as degree-marks. The frogs would climb to the top in fine weather, but keep to the bottom of the bottle in bad weather. It was Grandfather's plan to consult his frogs before going out on picnics.

But to return to my own pond....

I soon grew into the habit of visiting it on my own, to explore its banks and shallows; and, taking off my shoes, I would wade into the muddy water up to my knees, and pluck the water-lilies off the surface.

One day, when I reached the pond, I found it already occupied by the buffaloes. Their owner, a boy a little older than I, was swimming about in the middle of the pond. Instead of climbing out on to the bank, he would pull himself up on the back of one of his buffaloes, stretch his naked brown body out on the animal's glistening back, and start singing to himself.

When the boy saw me staring at him from across the pond, he smiled, showing gleaming white teeth in his dark, sun-burned face. He invited me to join him in a swim. I told him I could not swim, and he offered to teach me. He dived off the back of his buffalo and swam across to me. And I, having removed my shirt and shorts, followed his instructions until I was struggling about among the water-lilies.

The boy's name was Ramu, and he promised to give me swimming lessons every afternoon. And so it was during the afternoons — especially summer afternoons when everyone else was asleep — that we met.

Very soon I was able to swim across the pond to sit with Ramu astride a contented buffalo, standing like an island in the middle of a muddy ocean. Ramu came from a family of farmers and had as yet received no schooling. But he was well-versed in folk-lore and knew a great deal about birds and animals.

I liked the buffaloes too. Sometimes we would try racing them, Ramu and I riding on different buffaloes. But they were lazy creatures, and would leave one comfortable spot only to look for another or, if they were in no mood for games, would roll over on their backs, taking us with them into the mud and green scum of the pond. I would often emerge from the pond in shades of green and khaki, then slip into the house through the bathroom, bathing under the tap before getting into·

my clothes.

Ramu and I sat on our favourite buffalo and watched a pair of sarus-cranes prancing and capering around each other: tall, stork-like birds with naked red heads and long red legs. They are always very devoted companions, and it is said that if a sarus is killed its mate will haunt the scene for weeks, calling sadly, and sometimes pining away and dying of grief. They are held in great affection by village people, and when caught young make excellent pets. Though Grandfather did not keep a sarus-crane, he said they were as good as watch-dogs, giving loud trumpet-like calls when they were disturbed.

"Many birds are sacred," said Ramu, as a blue-jay swooped down from the peepul tree and carried off a grasshopper. He told me that both the blue-jay and Lord Shiva were called *Nilkanth*. Shiva had a blue throat, like the bird, because out of compassion for the human race, He had swallowed a deadly poison meant to destroy the world. Keeping the poison in His throat, He did not let it go down any farther.

"Are squirrels sacred?" I asked.

"Lord Krishna loved squirrels," said Ramu. "He would take them in His arms and stroke them with His long fingers. That is why they have four dark lines down their backs from head to tail. Krishna was very dark, and the lines are the marks of His fingers."

It seemed that both Ramu and Grandfather were of the opinion that we should be more gentle with birds and animals, and not kill so many of them.

"It is also important that we respect them," said Grand-

180

father. "We must acknowledge their rights on the earth. Everywhere, birds and animals are finding it more difficult to live because we are destroying their forests. They have to keep moving as the trees disappear."

Ramu and I spent many long summer afternoons at the pond. Only the buffaloes and the frogs and the saruscranes knew of our friendship. They had accepted us as part of their own world, their muddy but comfortable pond. And when finally I went away, both they and Ramu must have assumed that I would return like the birds.

The Banyan Tree

Though the house and grounds belonged to my grandparents, the magnificent old banyan tree was mine — chiefly because Grandfather, at sixty-five, could no longer climb it.

Its spreading branches, which hung to the ground and took root again, forming a number of twisting passages, gave me endless pleasure. Among them were squirrels and snails and butterflies. The tree was older than the house, older than Grandfather, as old as Dehra Dun itself. I could hide myself in its branches, behind thick green leaves, and spy on the world below.

My first friend was a small grey squirrel. Arching his back and sniffing into the air, he seemed at first to resent my invasion of his privacy. But when he found that I did not arm myself with catapult or air-gun, he became friendly, and when I started bringing him pieces of cake and biscuit, he grew quite bold and was soon taking morsels from my hand.

Before long he was delving into my pockets and helping himself to whatever he could find. He was a very young squirrel, and his friends and relatives probably thought him foolish and headstrong for trusting a human.

In the spring, when the banyan tree was full of small red figs, birds of all kinds would flock into its branches: the red-bottomed bulbul, cheerful and greedy; gossipy rosy-pastors; parrots, mynas and crows squabbling with one another. During the fig season, the banyan tree was the noisiest place in the garden.

Half way up the tree I had built a crude platform where I would spend the afternoons when it was not too hot. I could read there, propping myself up against the bole of the tree with a cushion from the living-room. *Treasure Island, Huckleberry Finn* and *The Story of Dr. Dolittle* were some of the books that made up my banyan tree library.

When I did not feel like reading, I could look down through the leaves at the world below. And on one particular afternoon I had a grand-stand view of that classic of the Indian wilds, a fight between a mongoose and a cobra. And this one had not been staged for my benefit!

The warm breezes of approaching summer had sent everyone, including the gardener, into the house. I was feeling drowsy myself, wondering if I should go to the pond and have a swim with Ramu and the buffaloes, when I saw a huge black cobra gliding out of a clump of cactus. At the same time a mongoose emerged from the bushes and went straight for the cobra.

In a clearing beneath the banyan tree, in bright sunshine, they came face to face.

The cobra knew only too well that the grey mongoose,

183

three feet long, was a superb fighter, clever and aggressive. But the cobra, too, was a skilful and experienced fighter. He could move swiftly and strike with the speed of light; and the sacks behind his long sharp fangs were full of deadly poison.

It was to be a battle of champions.

Hissing defiance, his forked tongue darting in and out, the cobra raised three of his six feet off the ground, and spread his broad, spectacled hood. The mongoose bushed his tail. The long hair on his spine stood up.

Though the combatants were unaware of my presence in the tree, they were soon made aware of the arrival of two other spectators. One was a myna, the other a jungle crow. They had seen these preparations for battle, and had settled on the cactus to watch the outcome. Had they been content only to watch, all would have been well with both of them.

The cobra stood on the defensive, swaying slowly from side to side, trying to mesmerise the mongoose into making a false move. But the mongoose knew the power of his opponent's glassy, unwinking eyes, and refused to meet them. Instead he fixed his gaze at a point just below the cobra's hood, and opened the attack.

Moving forward quickly until he was just within the cobra's reach, the mongoose made a pretended move to one side. Immediately the cobra struck. His great hood came down so swiftly that I thought nothing could save the mongoose. But the little fellow jumped neatly to one side, and darted in as swiftly as the cobra, biting the snake on the back and darting away again out of reach.

At the same moment that the cobra struck, the crow and the myna hurled themselves at him, only to collide heavily in mid-air. Shrieking insults at each other, they returned to the cactus plant.

A few drops of blood glistened on the cobra's back.

The cobra struck again and missed. Again the mongoose sprang aside, jumped in and bit. Again the birds dived at the snake, bumped into each other instead, and returned shrieking to the safety of the cactus.

The third round followed the same course as the first but with one dramatic difference. The crow and the myna, still determined to take part in the proceedings, dived at the cobra; but this time they missed each other as well as their mark. The myna flew on and reached its perch, but the crow tried to pull up in mid-air and turn back. In the second that it took the bird to do this, the cobra whipped his head back and struck with great force, his snout thudding against the crow's body.

I saw the bird flung nearly twenty feet across the garden. It fluttered about for a while, then lay still. The myna remained on the cactus plant, and when the snake and the mongoose returned to the fight, very wisely decided not to interfere again!

The cobra was weakening, and the mongoose, walking fearlessly up to it, raised himself on his short legs and with a lightning snap had the big snake by the snout. The cobra writhed and lashed about in a frightening manner, and even coiled itself about the mongoose, but to no avail. The little fellow hung grimly on, until the snake had ceased to struggle. He then smelt along its quivering length, gripped it round the hood, and dragged it into the bushes.

The myna dropped cautiously to the ground, hopped about, peered into the bushes from a safe distance, and then, with a shrill cry of congratulation, flew away.

The banyan tree was also the setting for what we were to call the Strange Case of the Grey Squirrel and the White Rat.

The white rat was Grandfather's — he had bought it for one-quarter of a rupee — but I would often take it with me into the banyan tree, where it soon struck up a friendship with one of the squirrels. They would go off together on little excursions among the roots and branches of the old tree.

Then the squirrel started building a nest. At first she tried building it in my pockets, and when I went indoors and took off my clothes I would find straw and grass falling out.

Then one day Grandmother's knitting was missing. We hunted for it everywhere but without success.

The next day I saw something glinting in a hole in the banyan tree. Going up to investigate, I saw that it was the end of Grandmother's steel knitting-needle. On looking further, I discovered that the hole was crammed with knitting. Amongst the wool were three baby squirrels — and all of them were white!

We gazed at the white squirrels in wonder and fascination. Grandfather was puzzled at first, but when I told him about the white rat's visits to the tree, his brow cleared. He said the white rat must be the father.

186

A Crow in the House

The young crow had fallen from its nest and was fluttering about on the road, in danger of being crushed by a cart or a tonga, or seized by a cat, when I picked it up and brought it home. It was in a sorry condition, beak gaping and head dropping, and we did not expect it to live. But Grandfather and I did our best to bring it round. We fed it by prising its beak gently open with a pencil, pushing in a little bread and milk, and then removing the pencil to allow it to swallow. We varied this diet with occasional doses of Grandmother's home-made plum wine, and as a result the young crow was soon on the road to recovery.

He was offered his freedom but he did not take it. Instead he made himself at home in the house. Grandmother, Aunt Mabel, and even some of Grandfather's pets objected; but there was no way of getting rid of the bird. He took over the administration of the house.

We were not sure that he was male, but we called him Caesar.

Before long, Caesar was joining us at meal times, besides finding his own grubs or beetles in the garden. He

187

danced about on the dining table and gave us no peace until he had been given his small bowl of meat and soup and vegetables. He was always restless, fidgeting about, investigating things. He would hop across a table to empty a match-box of its contents, or rip the daily paper to shreds, or overturn a vase of flowers, or tug at the tail of one of the dogs.

"That crow will be the ruin of us!" grumbled Grand-mother, picking marigolds off the carpet. "Can't you keep him in a cage?"

We did try keeping Caesar in a cage, but he was so angry, and objected with such fierce cawing and flapping, that it was better for our nerves and peace of mind to give him the run of the house. He did not show any inclination to join the other crows in the banyan tree. Grandfather said this was because he was really a jungle crow — a raven of sorts — and probably felt a little contemptuous of very ordinary carrion crows. But it seemed to me that Caesar, having grown used to living with humans on equal terms, had become snobbish and did not wish to mix with his own kind. He would even squabble with· Harold the Hornbill. Perching on top of Harold's cage, he would peck at the big bird's feet, whereupon Harold would swear and scold and try to catch Caesar through the bars.

In time, Caesar learnt to talk a little — as ravens some-times do — in a cracked, throaty voice. He would sit for hours outside the window, banging on the glass with his beak and calling, *"Hello, hello."* He seemed to recognise the click of the gate when I came home from school, and would come to the door with a hop, skip and jump, saying, *"Hello, hello!"* I had also taught him to sit on my arm and say *"Kiss, kiss"*, while he placed his head gently against my mouth.

On one of Aunt Mabel's visits, Caesar alighted on her arm and cackled, *"Kiss, kiss!"* Aunt Mabel was delighted — and possibly flattered — and leant forward for a kiss. But Caesar's attention shifted to my aunt's gleaming spectacles, and thrusting at them with his beak, he knocked them off. Aunt Mabel never was a success with the pets.

Pet or pest? Grandmother insisted that Caesar was a pest, in spite of his engaging habits. If he had restricted his activities to our own house, it would not have been so bad; but he took to visiting neighbouring houses and stealing pens and pencils, hair-ribbons, combs, keys, shuttlecocks, toothbrushes and false teeth. He was especially fond of toothbrushes, and made a collection of them on top of the cupboard in my room. Most of the neighbours were represented in our house by a toothbrush. Toothbrush sales went up that year. So did Grandmother's blood-pressure.

Caesar spied on children going into the *bania's* shop, and often managed to snatch sweets from them as they came out. Clothes pegs fascinated him. Neighbours would return from the bazar to find their washing lying in the mud, and no sign of the pegs. These, too, found their way to the top of my cupboard.

It was Caesar's gardening activities that finally led to disaster. He was helping himself to our neighbour's beans when a stick was flung at him, breaking his leg. I

189

carried the unfortunate bird home, and Grandfather and I washed and bandaged his leg as best we could. But it would not mend. Caesar hung his head and no longer talked. He grew weaker day by day, refusing to eat. An occasional sip of Grandmother's home-made wine was all that kept him going.

One morning I found him dead on the sofa, his legs stiff in the air. Poor Caesar! His anti-social habits had led to his early end.

I dug a shallow grave in the garden, and buried him there, along with all the toothbrushes and clothes pegs he had taken so much trouble to collect.

Henry: a Chameleon

This is the story of Henry, our pet chameleon. Chameleons are in a class by themselves, and are no ordinary reptiles. From their nearest relatives, the lizards, they are easily distinguished by certain outstanding marks. A chameleon's tongue is as long as its body. On its head is a rigid crest which looks like a fireman's helmet. His limbs are long and slender, and his fingers and toes are more developed than those of other reptiles.

Henry's most remarkable characteristics were his eyes. They were not beautiful. But his left eye was quite independent of his right. He could move one eye without disturbing the other. This gave him a horrible squint. Each eye-ball, raised out of his head, was wobbled up and down, backwards and forwards, quite independently of its partner. Reptiles are not gifted like us with binocular vision. They do not see an object with both eyes at once.

Whenever I visited Henry, he would treat me with great caution, sitting perfectly still on his perch with his back to me. But his nearest eye would move round like the beam of a searchlight until it had got me well in focus.

Then it would stop, and the other eye would proceed to carry out an independent survey of its own in some different direction. Henry took nobody on trust, and treated my friendliest gestures with grave suspicion.

Tiring of his attitude, I would tickle him gently in the ribs with my finger. This always threw him into a great rage. He would blow himself up to an enormous size, his lungs filling his body with air. He would sit up on his hind legs, swaying from side to side, hoping to overawe me. Opening his mouth very wide, he would let out an angry hiss. But his protests went no further. He did not bite. Non-violence was his creed.

Many people believe the chameleon is a dangerous and poisonous reptile. When Grandfather was visiting a friend in the country, he came upon a noisy scene at the garden gate. Men were shouting, hurling stones and brandishing sticks. The cause of all this was a chameleon who had been discovered sunning himself on a shrub. The gardener declared that it was a thing capable of poisoning people at a distance of twenty feet, and as a result the entire household had risen in arms. Grandfather was in time to save the chameleon from certain death, and brought the little reptile home.

That chameleon was Henry and that was how he came to live with us.

Henry was a harmless creature. If I put my finger in his mouth even in his wildest moments he would simply wait for me to take it out again. I suppose he could bite. His rigid jaws carried a number of fine pointed teeth. But Henry was rightly convinced that these were given to him solely for the purpose of chewing his food.

Provided I was patient, Henry was willing to take food from my hands. This he did very swiftly. His tongue was a sort of boomerang which came back to him with the food, an insect victim, attached to it. Before I could realise what had happened, the grasshopper held between my fingers would be lodged between Henry's jaws.

Henry did not cause any trouble in our house, but he did create something like a riot in the nursery school down the road.

It happened like this.

When the papayas in our garden were ripe, Grandmother usually sent a basket of them to her friend, Mrs. Ghosh, who was the principal of the nursery school. On this occasion, Henry managed to smuggle himself into the basket of papayas when no one was looking. (He did have a cage of his own, but was seldom in it.) The gardener dutifully carried the papayas across to the school and left them in Mrs. Ghosh's office. When Mrs. Ghosh came in after making her rounds, she began admiring and examining the papayas. Out popped Henry.

Mrs. Ghosh screamed. Henry would probably have liked to blush a deep red, but he turned a bright green instead, as that was the colour of the papayas. Mrs. Ghosh's assistant, Miss Daniels, rushed in, took one look at the chameleon, and joined in the screaming. Henry took fright and fled from the office, running down the corridor and into one of the classrooms. There he climbed on to a desk, while children ran in all directions, some to get away from Henry, some to catch him. But

193

Henry made his exit from a window, and disappeared in the garden.

Grandmother heard all about the incident from Mrs. Ghosh, but did not tell her the chameleon was ours. I did not think Henry would find his way back to us, because the school was three houses away. But three days later, I found him sunning himself on the garden wall. He readily accepted some food from my hand, and allowed himself to be recaptured.

A Week in the Jungle

Grandfather never hunted wild animals, he couldn't understand the pleasure some people obtained from killing the creatures of our forests. Birds and animals, he felt, had as much right to live as humans. We could kill them for food, he said, because even animals killed for food; but not for pleasure.

At the age of twelve I did not have the same high principles as Grandfather. Nevertheless, I disliked shooting. I found it boring.

Uncle Henry and some of his sporting friends once took me on a shikar expedition into the Terai jungles in the Siwaliks. The prospect of a week in the jungle, as camp-follower to several adults with guns, filled me with dismay. I knew that long, weary hours would be spent tramping behind these tall, professional-looking huntsmen who spoke in terms of bagging this tiger or that wild elephant, when all they ever got, if they were lucky, was a wild hare or a partridge. Tigers and excitement, it seemed, came only to Jim Corbett.

This particular expedition proved to be no different

from others. There were four men with guns, and at the end of the week all that they had shot were two miserable, underweight wild fowl. But I managed, on our second day in the jungle, to be left behind in the rest-house. And, in the course of a morning's exploration of the old bungalow, I discovered a shelf of books half-hidden in a corner of the back verandah.

Who had left them there? A literary forest officer? A *memsahib* who had been bored by her husband's camp-fire boasting? Or someone who had no interest in the "manly" sport of slaughtering wild animals and had brought his library along to pass the time? He must have left it behind for others like him.

Or possibly the poor fellow had gone into the jungle one day, as a gesture to his more blood-thirsty companions, and been trampled by an elephant, or gored by a wild boar, or (more likely) accidentally shot by one of the shikaris — and his sorrowing friends had taken his remains away and left his books behind.

Anyway, there they were — a shelf of some thirty volumes, in different shapes, sizes and colours. I wiped the thick dust off the covers and examined the titles. As my reading tastes had not yet formed, I was willing to try anything. The bookshelf was varied in its contents — and my own interests have since remained fairly universal.

On that second day in the forest rest-house, I discovered P.G. Wodehouse and read his *Love Among the Chickens,* an early Ukridge story and still one of my favourites. By the time the perspiring hunters came home in the evening, with their spent cartridges and impressive·

196

excuses, I had made a start with M.R. James' *Ghost Stories of an Antiquary*. This kept me awake most of the night, until the oil in the kerosene lamp was exhausted.

Next morning, fresh and optimistic again, the shikaris set out for a different area, where they hoped to get a tiger. They had employed a party of villagers to beat the jungle, and all day I could hear the tom-toms throbbing in the distance. This did not prevent me from finishing M.R. James, or discovering a little book called *A Naturalist on the Prowl* by 'EHA'. It described the tremendous fun and interest to be had from studying the wild life in one's own back garden — the grasshoppers, beetles, ants, butterflies and praying-mantises, all living such fascinating lives just outside (and sometimes inside) our bedroom windows.

Before I had finished the book, I was looking for spiders in the corners of the old bungalow and stalking grasshoppers in the long grass of the compound. My concentration was disturbed only once, when I looked up and saw a spotted deer crossing the open space in front of the house. The deer disappeared among the *sal* trees, and I returned to the verandah and my book.

Dusk had fallen when I heard the party returning from the hunt. The hunters were talking loudly and seemed excited. Perhaps they had got their tiger. I put down my book and came out of the house to meet them.

"Did you get the tiger?" I asked excitedly.

"No, laddie," said Uncle Henry. "I think we'll get it tomorrow. But you should have been with us — we saw a spotted deer!"

197

There were three days left, and I knew I would never get through the entire bookshelf. This I did not intend doing, as not all the authors on the shelf appealed to me. I chose at random *The Wind in the Willows, The Jungle Book* and *David Copperfield*.

On the day I made the literary acquaintance of Mowgli, the wolf-boy, the shikaris shot the two wild fowl already mentioned. As the party had from the first intended living off the jungle, only some tinned foods had been brought along; but two lean birds were insufficient for a party of five, and once again the meal consisted mostly of corned meat and mustard.

Next day, while the grown-ups were looking for their tiger and I was learning wisdom from the Water Rat, Toad and other river people of *The Wind in the Willows,* an event took place which disturbed my reading for a little while.

I had noticed, on the previous day, that a number of stray mongrels — belonging to watchmen, villagers and forest-guards — always hung about the house, waiting for scraps of food to be thrown away. It was ten o'clock in the morning (a time when wild animals seldom come into the open), when I heard a sudden yelp in the clearing. Looking up, I saw a full-grown panther making off into the jungle with one of the dogs held in its mouth. The panther had either been driven towards the house by the beaters, or had watched the party leave the bungalow and decided to help itself to a meal.

There was no one else about at the time. Since the dog was obviously dead within seconds of being seized, and the panther had disappeared, I saw no point in raising an alarm but returned to my book.

It was getting late when the shikaris returned. They were dirty, sweaty, and, as usual, disappointed. This time their excuses held a note of defiance. They took their corned meat in silence. Next day we were to return to "civilization," and none of the hunters had anything to show for a week in the jungles of India.

"No game left in these jungles," said the leading member of the party, famed for once having shot two man-eating tigers and a basking crocodile in rapid succession.

"It's the weather," said another. "No rain at all this winter."

"Don't know what the country's coming to," grumbled the third.

"I saw a panther this morning," I said modestly.

In fact, I was altogether too modest. I might just as well have said, "I saw a donkey this morning," for all the impression I made.

"Did you really?" said the leading hunter. He glanced at the book lying beside me. "Young Master Copperfield says he saw a panther!"

The others were only faintly amused. They did not have the energy to laugh.

"Too imaginative for his age," said one of them. "Comes from reading so much, I suppose."

"If you were to get out of the house and into the jungle a little," said Uncle Henry reproachfully, "you might really see a panther."

"Don't know what young fellows are coming to these days..."

"Why didn't you grab it, man, and take it to Grand-father?" And everyone laughed.

I went to bed early and left them to their tales of the "good old days" when rhinos, cheetahs and possibly even the legendary phoenix were still available for slaughter.

I came home with a poor reputation. My uncle's friends thought I was both a sissy and a liar. And Uncle Henry, poor man, seemed to think I was responsible for the failure of the entire expedition. He did not take me with him again. But Grandfather, when I told him all about the hunt, doubled up with laughter and said he wished he had been with us, if only to see the faces of Uncle Henry and his friends. As a measure of his delight, he bought me a copy of *David Copperfield,* for I had not been able to finish the one in the forest rest-house. I finally got through it in the banyan tree, in the company of several squirrels and a very noisy cicada.

A Photograph

Grandmother sat in a rocking-chair, under the mango tree. It was late summer and there were sunflowers in the garden and a warm wind in the trees. Grandmother was knitting me a pullover for the winter months. Her hair was white, her eyes were not very strong, but her fingers moved quickly with the needles, and the needles kept clicking all afternoon. Grandmother was old, but there were very few wrinkles on her skin.

In some of my tales I have perhaps been guilty of writing more admiringly of Grandfather than of Grandmother. It's true that Grandfather and I had much in common, and that he gave me more of his time; but then, he had more time to give. He was a retired gentleman. But housewives never retire. And Grandmother always had housework. She saw to our meals, she did the shopping, kept the household accounts, and dealt with a variety of tradesmen including the butcher, the baker, the *dhobi*, and various egg, fruit, vegetable and charcoal vendors.

And so, if our pets sometimes hindered her in the

efficient running of the house, who can blame her for being a little short with us at times?

In the long run, though Grandmother grumbled, she always tolerated most of our pets. She nursed Toto the monkey when he was sick; she was fond of the Hornbill; in fact, she liked all birds. She kept her own bird-bath in the garden, where mynas, thrushes, bulbuls and flower-peckers would come for a dip or a drink, and she never forgot to fill the stone bath with fresh water in the mornings.

When she did find time to relax in her rocking-chair, she liked having me beside her, and she liked talking about her youth.

One afternoon, after lunch (or tiffin, as we called it then), I was rummaging in a box of old books and family heirlooms that I had found in the box room. There was not much to interest me except a book on butterflies, and as I was going through it I found a small photograph in between the pages. It was a faded picture, a little yellow and foggy — a picture of a girl standing against a wall; and from the other side of the wall a pair of hands reached up, as though someone were about to climb over it. There were flowers growing near the girl, but I could not tell what they were; there was a small tree, too, but it was just a tree to me.

I ran out into the garden.

"Granny!" I shouted. "Look at this picture! I found it in that box of old things. Whose picture is it?"

I raised myself on the arm of the rocking-chair, and we nearly toppled over into a bed of nasturtiums.

"Now look what you've gone and done," said Grandmother. "I've lost count of my stitches. The next time you jump up like that, I'll make you finish the pullover yourself."

Grandmother was always threatening to teach me how to knit. She said it would take my mind off unhealthy creatures like frogs and lizards and buffaloes. Once, when Toto tore the drawing room curtains, she put a needle and thread in my hand and made me stitch the curtain together, even though I made long, two-inch stitches which had to be taken out by Grandmother and done all over again.

She took the photograph from my hand, and we both stared at it for quite some time. The girl had long, loose hair, and she wore a long dress that nearly covered her ankles, and sleeves that reached her wrists; but, in spite of all this drapery, the girl appeared to be full of freedom and movement; she stood with her legs apart and her hands on her hips, and she had a wide, almost devilish smile on her face.

"Whose picture is it?" I asked.

"A little girl's, of course," said Grandmother. "Can't you tell?"

"Yes, but did you know her?"

"Oh yes, I knew her," said Grandmother. "But she was a wicked little girl, and I shouldn't tell you about her. I'll tell you about the photograph. It was taken in our home, oh many many years ago, and that's the garden wall, and over the wall there was a road leading to town. That girl used to sneak over the wall sometimes, and visit the bazar.

She couldn't resist *jilebis*. Do you like *jilebis*?"

"Yes, very much! But whose hands are they?" I asked. "Coming up from the other side?"

Grandmother squinted and looked closely at the picture, shaking her head. "It's the first time I've noticed," she said. "They must have been a child's, another child's."

"Were they Grandfather's? Didn't he climb over the wall, afterwards?"

"No, nobody climbed up. At least, I don't remember."

"And you remember well, Granny."

"Yes, I remember ... I remember what is not in the photograph. It was a spring day, and there was a cool breeze blowing. Those flowers at the girl's feet, they were marigolds, and the bougainvillaea creeper was a mass of purple. You can't see those colours in the photo, and even if you could, you wouldn't be able to smell the flowers or feel the breeze."

"And what about the girl?" I asked. "Tell me about the girl."

"Well, she was a wicked girl," said Grandmother. "You don't know the trouble her mother had getting her into those fine clothes she's wearing."

"They're terrible clothes," I said.

"She thought so, too. Most of the time she hardly wore a thing. Dehra Dun summers were as hot then as they are now. She used to go swimming in the canal. The neighbours were shocked. Boys never teased her, because she didn't hesitate to fight them!"

"She looks tough," I said. " You can tell by the way she's

smiling. At any moment something's going to happen."

"Something *did* happen," said Grandmother. "Her mother wouldn't let her get out of those awful clothes, so she jumped into the canal fully clothed!"

I burst into laughter, and Grandmother joined in.

"Who was the girl?" I asked. "You must tell me who she was."

"No, that wouldn't do," said Grandmother. "I won't tell you."

I knew the girl in the photograph was really Grandmother, but I pretended not to know. I knew, because Grandmother still smiled in the same way.

"Come on, Granny," I said. "Tell me, tell me."

But Grandmother shook her head and carried on with her knitting; and I held the photograph in my hands, looking from it to my grandmother and back again, trying to find points in common between the old lady and the little pigtailed girl. A lemon-coloured butterfly settled on the end of Grandmother's knitting-needle, and stayed there while the needle clicked away. I made a grab at the butterfly, and it flew off in a dipping flight and settled on a sunflower.

"I wonder whose hands they were," whispered Grandmother to herself, with her head bowed in memory, and her needles clicking away in the soft, warm silence of that summer afternoon.

All this was many years ago.

When my parents returned to India, I left my grandparents' house and went to live in Saurashtra.

Grandfather and I corresponded regularly, and he kept me informed of his pets and any new additions to his zoo.

I often think about his birds and animals, the inhabitants of the banyan tree, and the residents of the pond behind the old house. And I remember Ramu the village boy, and the fun we had with the buffaloes. And I wish that I might see them again.

And perhaps one day when I have made some money I will go back to Dehra Dun and buy back Grandfather's old house and start another zoo of my own.

The Road to the Bazaar

It was almost noon, and the jungle was very still, very silent. Heat waves shimmered along the railway embankment where it cut a path through the tall evergreen trees. The railway lines were two straight black serpents disappearing into the tunnel in the hillside.

Suraj stood near the cutting, waiting for the midday train. It wasn't a station, and he wasn't catching a train. He was waiting so that he could watch the steam-engine come roaring out of the tunnel.

He had cycled out of Dehra and taken the jungle path until he had come to a small village. He had left the cycle there, and walked over a low, scrub-covered hill and down to the tunnel exit.

Now he looked up. He had heard, in the distance, the shrill whistle of the engine. He couldn't see anything, because the train was approaching from the other side of the hill; but presently a sound like distant thunder issued from the tunnel, and he knew the train was coming through.

A second or two later, the steam-engine shot out of the

209

tunnel, snorting and puffing like some green, black and gold dragon, some beautiful monster out of Suraj's dreams. Showering sparks left and right, it roared a challenge to the jungle.

Instinctively, Suraj stepped back a few paces. Waves of hot steam struck him in the face. Even the trees seemed to flinch from the noise and heat. And then the train had gone, leaving only a plume of smoke to drift lazily over the tall Shisham trees.

The jungle was still again. No one moved.

Suraj turned from his contemplation of the drifting smoke and began walking along the embankment towards the tunnel.

The tunnel grew darker as he walked further into it. When he had gone about twenty yards it became pitch black. Suraj had to turn and look back at the opening to reassure himself that there was still daylight outside. Ahead of him, the tunnel's other opening was just a small round circle of light.

The tunnel was still full of smoke from the train, but it would be several hours before another train came through. Till then, the cutting belonged to the jungle again.

Suraj didn't stop, because there was nothing to do in the tunnel and nothing to see. He had simply wanted to walk through, so that he would know what the inside of a tunnel was really like. The walls were damp and sticky. A bat flew past. A lizard scuttled between the lines.

Coming straight from the darkness into the light, Suraj was dazzled by the sudden glare and put a hand up to

210

shade his eyes. He looked up at the tree-covered hillside and thought he saw something moving between the trees.

It was just a flash of orange and gold, and a long swishing tail. It was there between the trees for a second or two, and then it was gone.

About fifteen metres from the entrance to the tunnel stood the watchman's hut. Marigolds grew in front of the hut, and at the back there was a small vegetable patch. It was the watchman's duty to inspect the tunnel and keep it clear of obstacles. Every day, before the train came through, he would walk the length of the tunnel. If all was well, he would return to his hut and take a nap. If something was wrong, he would walk back up the line and wave a red flag and the engine-driver would slow down. At night, the watchman lit an oil-lamp and made a similar inspection of the tunnel. Of course, he would not stop the train if there was a porcupine on the line. But if there was any danger to the train, he'd go back up the line and wave his lamp to the approaching engine. If all was well, he'd hang his lamp at the door of his hut and go to sleep.

He was just settling down on his cot for an afternoon nap when he saw the boy emerge from the tunnel. He waited until Suraj was only a metre or so away and then said: "Welcome, welcome, I don't often have visitors. Sit down for a while, and tell me why you were inspecting my tunnel."

"Is it your tunnel?" asked Suraj.

211

"It is," said the watchman. "It is truly my tunnel, since no one else will have anything to do with it. I have only lent it to the Government."

Suraj sat down on the edge of the cot.

"I wanted to see the train come through," he said. "And then, when it had gone, I thought I'd walk through the tunnel."

"And what did you find in it?"

"Nothing. It was very dark. But when I came out, I thought I saw an animal — up on the hill — but I'm not sure, it moved off very quickly."

"It was a leopard you saw," said the watchman. "My leopard."

"Do you own a leopard too?"

"I do."

"And do you lend it to the Government?"

"I do not."

"Is it dangerous?"

"No, it's a leopard that minds its own business. It comes to this range for a few days every month."

"Have you been here a long time?" asked Suraj.

"Many years. My name is Sunder Singh."

"My name's Suraj."

"There is one train during the day. And there is one train during the night. Have you seen the night-mail come through the tunnel?"

"No. At what time does it come?"

"About nine o'clock, if it isn't late. You could come and sit here with me, if you like. And after it has gone, instead of going to sleep I will take you home."

"I'll ask my parents," said Suraj. "Will it be safe?"

"Of course. It is safer in the jungle than in the town. Nothing happens to me out here. But last month, when I went into town, I was almost run over by a bus."

Sunder Singh yawned and stretched himself out on the cot. "And now I am going to take a nap, my friend. It is too hot to be up and about in the afternoon."

"Everyone goes to sleep in the afternoon," complained Suraj. "My father lies down as soon as he's had his lunch."

"Well, the animals also rest in the heat of the day. It is only the tribe of boys who cannot, or will not, rest."

Sunder Singh placed a large banana-leaf over his face to keep away the flies, and was soon snoring gently. Suraj stood up, looking up and down the railway tracks. Then he began walking back to the village.

The following evening, towards dusk, as the flying foxes swooped silently out of the trees, Suraj made his way to the watchman's hut.

It had been a long hot day, but now the earth was cooling, and a light breeze was moving through the trees. It carried with it the scent of mango blossoms, the promise of rain.

Sunder Singh was waiting for Suraj. He had watered his small garden, and the flowers looked cool and fresh. A kettle was boiling on a small oil-stove.

"I am making tea," he said. "There is nothing like a glass of hot tea while waiting for a train."

They drank their tea, listening to the sharp notes of the tailor-bird and the noisy chatter of the seven-sisters.

As the brief twilight faded, most of the birds fell silent. Sunder Singh lit his oil-lamp and said it was time for him to inspect the tunnel. He moved off towards the tunnel, while Suraj sat on the cot, sipping his tea. In the dark, the trees seemed to move closer to him. And the night-life of the forest was conveyed on the breeze — the sharp call of a barking deer, the cry of a fox, the quaint *tonk-tonk* of a nightjar. There were some sounds that Suraj didn't recognise — sounds that came from the trees, creakings and whisperings, as though the trees were coming to life, stretching their limbs in the dark, shifting a little, flexing their fingers.

Sunder Singh stood inside the tunnel, trimming his lamp. The night sounds were familiar to him and he did not give them much thought; but something else — a padded footfall, a rustle of dry leaves — made him stand still for a few seconds, peering into the darkness. Then, humming softly to himself, he returned to where Suraj was waiting. Ten minutes remained for the night-mail to arrive.

As Sunder Singh sat down on the cot beside Suraj, a new sound reached both of them quite distinctly — a rhythmic sawing sound, as of someone cutting through the branch of a tree.

"What's that?" whispered Suraj.

"It's the leopard," said Sunder Singh. "I think it's in the tunnel."

"The train will soon be here," said Suraj.

"Yes, my friend. And if we don't drive the leopard out of the tunnel, it will be run over and killed. I can't let that

216

happen."

"But won't it attack us if we try to drive it out?" asked Suraj, beginning to share the watchman's concern.

"Not this leopard. It knows me well. We have seen each other many times. It has a weakness for goats and stray dogs, but it will not harm us. Even so, I'll take my axe with me. You stay here, Suraj."

"No, I'm coming with you. It will be better than sitting here alone in the dark!"

"All right, but stay close behind me. And remember, there is nothing to fear."

Raising his lamp, Sunder Singh advanced into the tunnel, shouting at the top of his voice to try and scare away the animal. Suraj followed close behind; but he found he was unable to do any shouting. His throat was quite dry.

They had gone about twenty paces into the tunnel when the light from the lamp fell upon the leopard. It was crouching between the tracks, only five metres away from them. It was not a very big leopard, but it looked lithe and sinewy. Baring its teeth and snarling, it went down on its belly, tail twitching.

Suraj and Sunder Singh both shouted together. Their voices rang through the tunnel. And the leopard, uncertain as to how many terrifying humans were there in the tunnel with him, turned swiftly and disappeared into the darkness.

To make sure that it had gone, Sunder Singh and Suraj walked the length of the tunnel. When they returned to the entrance, the rails were beginning to hum. They knew the train was coming.

Suraj put his hand to one of the rails and felt its tremor. He heard the distant rumble of the train. And then the engine came round the bend, hissing at them, scattering sparks into the darkness, defying the jungle as it roared through the steep sides of the cutting. It charged straight at the tunnel, and into it, thundering past Suraj like the beautiful dragon of his dreams.

And when it had gone, the silence returned and the forest seemed to breathe, to live again. Only the rails still trembled with the passing of the train.

They trembled again to the passing of the same train, almost a week later, when Suraj and his father were both travelling in it.

Suraj's father was scribbling in a notebook, doing his accounts. Suraj sat at an open window staring out at the darkness. His father was going to Delhi on a business trip and had decided to take the boy along. ("I don't know where he gets to, most of the time," he'd complained. "I think it's time he learnt something about my business.")

The night-mail rushed through the forest with its hundreds of passengers. The carriage wheels beat out a steady rhythm on the rails. Tiny flickering lights came and went, as they passed small villages on the fringe of the jungle.

Suraj heard the rumble as the train passed over a small bridge. It was too dark to see the hut near the cutting, but he knew they must be approaching the tunnel. He strained his eyes looking out into the night; and then, just as the engine let out a shrill whistle, Suraj saw the lamp.

He couldn't see Sunder Singh, but he saw the lamp,

218

and he knew that his friend was out there.

The train went into the tunnel and out again; it left the jungle behind and thundered across the endless plains. Suraj stared out at the darkness, thinking of the lonely cutting in the forest and the watchman with the lamp who would always remain a firefly for those travelling thousands as he lit up the darkness for steam-engines and leopards.

The Big Race

Dawn crept quietly over the sleeping town. Only a cock was aware of it, and crowed. Koki heard a soft tapping on the window-pane, and immediately sat up in bed. She was ten years old. Her hair fell about her shoulders in a disorderly fashion and her dark eyes were slightly ringed, but she was wide awake and listening. The tapping was repeated.

Koki got out of bed and tiptoed across to the window and unlatched it. Ranji was standing outside, looking somewhat disgruntled.

"Come on," he said. "It's nearly time."

Koki put a finger to her lips, for she did not want her parents and grandmother to wake up.

"You go and call Bhim," she whispered. "I'll meet you on the maidaan."

Ranji hurried off in the direction of Bhim's house, and Koki turned from the window and went to the dressing-table. She combed her hair carelessly and tied it roughly in a ribbon. She was excited and in a hurry, and had slept in her dress, which was very crushed. Now she was ready

220

to leave.

Very quietly, she pulled open a dressing-table drawer, and brought out a cardboard box in which were punctured little holes. She opened the lid of the box to see if Rajkumari was all right.

Rajkumari, a dumpy rhino beetle, was asleep on the core of an apple. Koki did not disturb her. She closed the box and, barefoot, crept out of the house through the back door.

As soon as she was outside, Koki broke into a run. She did not stop running until she reached the maidaan.

On the maidaan, the slanting rays of the early morning sun were just beginning to make emeralds of the dewdrops. Later in the day the grass would dry and be prickly to the feet, but now it was cool and soft. A group of boys had gathered at one corner of the maidaan, talking excitedly, and among them were Ranji and Bhim, a lanky, bespectacled boy of fourteen. Koki was the only girl among them.

Bhim's beetle was the favourite for the race. It was a large bamboo beetle, with a slim body and long, slender legs, rather like its master's. It was called 2001. Ranji's beetle was a Stone Carrier with what looked like a very long pair of whiskers. It was appropriately named Moocha (Moustaches). Koki's beetle was not half as big as the other two. Though she did not know how to tell its sex, she was sure it was a female and had called it Rajkumari — Princess.

There were only three entries. Betting wasn't strictly allowed, but the boys made a few quiet bets among themselves. The prize was a giant insect (there was some disagreement as to whether it was a beetle or an outsize cockroach), which was meant to enable the winner to breed racing beetles on a larger scale.

There was some confusion when Ranji's Moocha escaped from his box and took a preliminary canter over the grass; but he was soon caught and returned to his enclosure. Moocha appeared to be in good form; in fact, he would be tough competition for Bhim's 2001.

The course was about two metres long, the tracks fifteen centimetres wide. The tracks were fenced with strips of cardboard so that the contestants did not get in each other's way or leave the course altogether. They were held at the starting-post by another piece of cardboard, which would be placed behind them as soon as the race began — just to make sure that no one backed out.

A little Sikh boy in a yellow pyjama-suit was acting as starter, and he kept blowing his whistle for order and attention. When the onlookers saw that the race was about to begin, they fell silent. The little Sikh boy then announced the rules of the race: the contestants were not to be touched during the race, or blown at from behind, or enticed forward with bits of food. They could, however, be cheered on as loudly as anyone wished.

Moocha and 2001 were already at the starting-post, but Koki was giving Rajkumari a few words of advice. Rajkumari seemed reluctant to leave her apple-core and needed to be taken forcibly to the starting-post.

There was further delay when Moocha and 2001 got their horns and whiskers entangled. They had to be

222

separated and calmed down before being placed in their respective tracks. The race was about to start.

Koki knelt on the grass, very quiet and serious, looking from Rajkumari to the finishing-line and back again. Ranji was biting his finger-nails. Bhim's glasses had clouded over, and he had to keep taking them off and wiping them on his shirt. There was a hush amongst the dozen or so spectators.

"Pee-ee-eeep!" The little Sikh boy blew his whistle.

They were off!

Or rather, Moocha and 2001 were off. Rajkumari was still at the starting-post, wondering what had happened to her apple-core.

Everyone was cheering madly, and Ranji was jumping up and down, and Bhim's glasses had been knocked off. Moocha was going at a spanking rate. 2001 wasn't taking a great deal of interest in the proceedings, but he *was* moving, and anything could happen in a race like this.

Koki was on the verge of tears. All the coaching she had given Rajkumari seemed to be of no avail. Her beetle was still looking bewildered and hurt.

"Stop sulking," said Koki. "I won't keep you if you don't try."

Then Moocha stopped suddenly, less than a metre from the finishing-line. He seemed to be having trouble with his whiskers, and kept twitching them this way and that. 2001 was catching up slowly but surely, and both Ranji and Bhim were shouting themselves hoarse. Nobody paid any attention to Rajkumari, who was considered to be out of the race; but Koki was using all her

223

will-power to get her racer going.

As 2001 approached Moocha, he seemed to sense his rival's trouble, and stopped to find out what was the matter. They could not see each other over the cardboard fence, but otherwise appeared to be communicating very well. Ranji and Bhim were becoming quite frantic in their efforts to rally their faltering steeds, and the cheering on all sides was deafening.

Rajkumari, goaded with rage and frustration at having been deprived of her apple-core, now took it into her head to make a bid for liberty and new pastures, and rushed forward in great style.

Koki shouted with joy, but the others did not notice the new challenge until Rajkumari had drawn level with her conferring rivals. There was a gasp from the crowd as Rajkumari strode across the finishing-line in record time.

Everyone cheered the gallant outsider. Ranji and Bhim very sportingly shook Koki by the hand, congratulating her on Rajkumari's victory. The little Sikh boy in the yellow pyjama-suit blew his whistle for silence and presented Koki with her prize.

Koki gazed in rapture at the new beetle — or was it a cockroach? She stroked its back with her thumb. The insect didn't seem to mind. Then, lest Rajkumari should feel jealous, Koki closed the prize-box and, picking up her victorious beetle, returned her to the apple-core.

The crowd began to break up. Ranji decided that he would trim Moocha's whiskers before the next race, and Bhim thought 2001 was in need of a special diet.

"Just wait till next Sunday," said Ranji. "Then watch my Moocha leave the rest of you standing!"

Bhim said nothing. He looked very thoughtful. There were some new training methods which he was going to try out for next time.

Koki walked home, a cardboard box under each arm. Her thoughts were busy with the future. She would breed beetles (or would they be cockroaches?) until she had a stable of about twenty. Her racers would win every event, both here and in the next town. They might make her famous. Beetle-racing would become a national sport!

Meanwhile, she was happy, and Rajkumari was happy on the apple-core, and the new insect was just being an insect and did not know and did not care about anything except how to get out of that wretched box.

Ranji's Wonderful Bat

"How's that!" shouted the wicket-keeper, holding the ball up in his gloves.

"How's that!" echoed the slip-fielders.

"How?" growled the fast bowler, glaring at the umpire.

"Out!" said the umpire.

And Suraj, the captain of the school team, was walking slowly back to the 'pavilion' — which was really a tool-shed at the end of the field.

The score stood at 53 for 4 wickets. Another sixty runs had to be made for victory, and only one good batsman remained. All the rest were bowlers who couldn't be expected to make many runs.

It was Ranji's turn to bat.

He was the youngest member of the team, only eleven, but sturdy and full of pluck. As he walked briskly to the wicket, his unruly black hair was blown about by a cool breeze that came down from the hills.

Ranji had a good eye and strong wrists, and had made lots of runs in some of the minor matches. But in the last two inter-school games his scores had been poor, the highest being 12 runs. Now he was determined to make enough runs to take his side to victory.

Ranji took his guard and prepared to face the bowler. The fielders moved closer, in anticipation of another catch. The tall fast bowler scowled and began his long run. His arm whirled over, and the hard shiny red ball came hurtling towards Ranji.

Ranji was going to lunge forward and play the ball back to the bowler, but at the last moment he changed his mind and stepped back, intending to push the ball through the ring of fielders on his right or 'off' side. The ball swung in the air, shot off the grass and came through sharply to strike Ranji on his pads.

"How's that!" screamed the bowler, hopping about like a kangaroo.

"How!" shouted the wicket-keeper.

"How?" asked all the fielders.

The umpire slowly raised a finger.

"Out," he said.

And it was Ranji's turn to walk back to the tool-shed.

The match was won by the visiting team.

"Never mind," said Suraj, patting Ranji on the back. "You'll do better next time. You're out of form just now, that's all."

But their cricket coach was sterner.

"You'll have to make more runs in the next game," he told Ranji, "or you'll lose your place in the side!"

Avoiding the other players, Ranji walked slowly homewards, his head down, his hands in his pockets. He was very upset. He had been trying so hard and practising so regularly, but when an important game came along he failed to make a big score. It seemed that there was nothing he could do about it. But he loved playing cricket, and he couldn't bear the thought of being out of the school team.

On his way home he had to pass the clock tower where he often stopped at Mr Kumar's Sports Shop, to chat with the owner or look at all the things on the shelves: footballs, cricket balls, badminton rackets, hockey sticks, balls of various shapes and sizes — it was a wonderland where Ranji usually liked to linger.

But this was one day when he didn't feel like stopping. He looked the other way and was about to cross the road when Mr Kumar's voice stopped him.

"Hello, Ranji! Off in a hurry today? And why are you looking so sad?"

So Ranji had to stop and say "namaste". He couldn't ignore Mr Kumar, who had been so kind and helpful, always giving him advice on how to play different kinds of bowling. Mr Kumar had been a state player once, and had scored a century in a match against Tanzania. Now he was too old for first-class cricket, but he liked encouraging young players and he thought Ranji would make a good cricketer.

"What's the trouble?" he asked, as Ranji stepped into the shop. "Lost the game today?"

Ranji felt better as soon as he was inside the shop. Because Mr Kumar was so friendly, the sports goods also seemed friendly. The bats and balls and shuttle-cocks all seemed to want to be helpful.

228

"We lost the match," said Ranji.

"Never mind," said Mr Kumar. "Where would we be without losers? There wouldn't be any games without them — no cricket or football or hockey or tennis! No carom or marbles. No sports shop for me! Anyway, how many runs did you make?"

"None. I made a big round egg."

Mr Kumar rested his hand on Ranji's shoulder. "Never mind. All good players have a bad day now and then."

"But I haven't made a good score in my last three matches," said Ranji. "I'll be dropped from the team if I don't do something in the next game."

"Well, we can't have that happening," mused Mr Kumar. "Something will have to be done about it."

"I'm just unlucky," said Ranji.

"Maybe, maybe ... But in that case, it's time your luck changed."

"It's too late now," said Ranji.

"Nonsense. It's never too late. Now, you just come with me to the back of my shop and I'll see if I can do something about your luck."

Puzzled, Ranji followed Mr Kumar through the curtained partition at the back of the shop. He found himself in a badly lit room stacked to the ceiling with all kinds of old and secondhand sporting goods — torn football bladders, broken bats, rackets without strings, broken darts and tattered badminton nets.

Mr Kumar began examining a number of old cricket bats, and after a few minutes he said "Ah!" and picked up one of the bats and held it out to Ranji.

"This is it!" he said. "This is the luckiest of all my old bats. This is the bat I made a century with!" And he gave it a twirl and started hitting an imaginary ball to all corners of the room.

"Of course it's an old bat, but it hasn't lost any of its magic," said Mr Kumar, pausing in his stroke-making to recover his breath. He held it out to Ranji. "Here, take it! I'll lend it to you for the rest of the cricket season. You won't fail with it."

Ranji took the bat and gazed at it with awe and delight.

"Is it really the bat you made a century with?" he asked.

"It is," said Mr Kumar. "And it may get you a hundred runs too!"

Ranji spent a nervous week waiting for Saturday's match. His school team would be playing a strong side from another town. There was a lot of class work that week, so Ranji did not get much time to practise with the other boys. As he had no brothers or sisters, he asked Koki, the girl next door, to bowl to him in the garden. Koki bowled quite well, but Ranji liked to hit the ball hard — "just to get used to the bat," he told her — and she soon got tired of chasing the ball all over the garden.

At last Saturday arrived, bright and sunny and just right for cricket.

Suraj won the toss for the school and took first batting.

The opening batsmen put on thirty runs without being separated. The visiting fast bowlers couldn't do much. The spin bowlers came on, and immediately there was a change in the game. Two wickets fell in one over, and the

230

score was 33 for 2. Suraj made a few quick runs, then he too was out to one of the spinners, caught behind the wicket. The next batsman was clean bowled — 46 for 4 — and it was Ranji's turn to bat.

He walked slowly to the wicket. The fielders crowded round him. He took guard and prepared for the first ball.

The bowler took a short run and then the ball was twirling towards Ranji, looking as though it would spin away from his bat as he leant forward into his stroke.

And then a thrill ran through Ranji's arm as he felt the ball meet the springy willow of the bat.

Crack!

The ball, hit firmly with the middle of Ranji's bat, streaked past the helpless bowler and sped towards the boundary. Four runs!

The bowler was annoyed, with the result that his next ball was a loose full-toss. Ranji swung it to the on-side boundary for another four.

And that was only the beginning. Now Ranji began to play all the strokes he knew: late cuts and square cuts, straight drives, on-drives and off-drives. The rival captain tried all his bowlers, fast and spin, but none of them could remove Ranji, who sent the fielders scampering all over the field.

At the lunch break he had scored 40. And twenty minutes after lunch, when Suraj closed the innings, Ranji was not out with 58.

The rival team was bowled out for a poor score, and Ranji's school won the match.

On his way home Ranji stopped at Mr Kumar's shop to

give him the good news.

"We won!" he said. "And I made 53 — my highest score so far. It really is a lucky bat!"

"I told you so," said Mr Kumar, giving Ranji a warm handshake. "There'll be bigger scores yet."

Ranji went home in high spirits. He was so pleased that he stopped at the Jumna Sweet Shop and bought two luddoos for Koki. She liked cricket but she liked luddoos even more.

Mr Kumar was right. It was only the beginning of Ranji's success with the bat. In the next game he scored 40, and was out when he grew careless and allowed himself to be stumped by the wicket-keeper. The game that followed was a two-day match, and Ranji, who was now batting at No. 3, made 45 runs. He hit a number of boundaries before being caught. In the second innings, when the school team needed only 60 runs for victory, Ranji was batting with 25 when the winning runs were hit.

Everyone was pleased with him — his coach, his captain, Suraj and Mr Kumar ... but no one knew about the lucky bat. That was a secret between Ranji and Mr Kumar.

One evening, during an informal game on the maidaan, Ranji's friend Bhim slipped while running after the ball, and cut his hand on a sharp stone. Ranji took him to a doctor near the clock tower, where the wound was washed and bandaged. As it was getting late, he decided to go straight home. Usually he walked, but that evening he caught a bus near the clock tower.

When he got home, his mother brought him a cup of

tea and while he was drinking it, Koki walked in. The first thing she said was, "Ranji, where's your bat?"

"Oh, I must have left it on the maidaan when Bhim got hurt," said Ranji, starting up and spilling his tea. "I'd better go and get it now, or it will disappear."

"You can fetch it tomorrow," said his mother. "It's getting dark."

"I'll take a torch," said Ranji.

He was worried about the bat. Without it, his luck might desert him. He hadn't the patience to wait for a bus, and ran all the way to the maidaan.

The maidaan was deserted and there was no sign of the bat. And then Ranji remembered that he'd had it with him on the bus, after saying goodbye to Bhim at the clock tower. He must have left it on the bus!

Well, he'd never find it now. The bat was lost for ever. And on Saturday Ranji's school would be playing their last and most important match of the cricket season against a visiting team from Delhi.

Next day he was at Mr Kumar's shop, looking very sorry for himself.

"What's the matter?" asked Mr Kumar.

"I've lost the bat," said Ranji. "Your lucky bat. The one I made all those runs with! I left it on the bus. And the day after tomorrow we are playing the Delhi school, and I'll be out for a duck, and we'll lose our chance of being the school champions."

Mr Kumar looked a little anxious at first; then he smiled and said, "You can still make all the runs you want."

"But I don't have the bat any more," said Ranji.

"Any bat will do," said Mr Kumar.

"What do you mean?"

"I mean it's the batsman and not the bat that matters. Shall I tell you something? That old bat I gave you was no different from any other bat I've used. True, I made lots of runs with it, but I made runs with other bats too. I never depended on a special bat for my runs. A bat has magic only when the batsman has magic! What you needed was *confidence*, not a bat. And by believing in the bat, you got your confidence back!"

"What's confidence?" asked Ranji. It was a new word for him.

"Con - fi - dence," said Mr Kumar slowly. "Confidence is knowing you are good."

"And I can be good without the bat?"

"Of course. You have always been good. You are good now. You will be good the day after tomorrow. Remember that. If you remember it, you'll make the runs."

On Saturday Ranji walked to the wicket with a bat borrowed from Bhim.

The school team had lost its first wicket with only 2 runs on the board. Ranji went in at this stage. The Delhi school's opening bowler was sending down some really fast ones. Ranji faced up to him.

The first ball was very fast but it wasn't on a good length. Quick on his feet, Ranji stepped back and pulled it hard to the on-boundary. The ball soared over the heads of the fielders and landed with a crash in crate full of cold-drink bottles.

A six! Everyone stood up and cheered.

And it was only the beginning of Ranji's wonderful innings.

The match ended in a draw, but Ranji's 75 was the talk of the school.

On his way home he bought a dozen luddoos. Six for Koki — and six for Mr Kumar.

The Long Day

Suraj was awakened by the sound of his mother busying herself in the kitchen. He lay in bed, looking through the open window at the sky getting lighter and the dawn pushing its way into the room. He knew there was something important about this new day, but for some time he couldn't remember what it was. Then, as the room cleared, his mind cleared. His school report would be arriving in the post.

Suraj knew he had failed. The class teacher had told him so. But his mother would only know of it when she read the report, and Suraj did not want to be in the house when she received it. He was sure it would be arriving today. So he had told his mother that he would be having his midday meal with his friend Somi — Somi, who wasn't even in town at the moment — and would be home only for the evening meal. By that time, he hoped, his mother would have recovered from the shock. He was glad his father was away on tour.

He slipped out of bed and went to the kitchen. His mother was surprised to see him up so early.

236

"I'm going for a walk, Ma," he said, "and then I'll go on to Somi's house."

"Well, have your bath first and put something in your stomach."

Suraj went to the tap in the courtyard and took a quick bath. He put on a clean shirt and shorts. Carelessly he brushed his thick, curly hair, knowing he couldn't bring much order to its wildness. Then he gulped down a glass of milk and hurried out of the house. The postman wouldn't arrive for a couple of hours, but Suraj felt that the earlier his start the better. His mother was surprised and pleased to see him up and about so early.

Suraj was out on the maidaan and still the sun had not risen. The maidaan was an open area of grass, about a hundred square metres, and from the middle of it could be seen the mountains, range upon range of them, stepping into the sky. A game of football was in progress, and one of the players called out to Suraj to join them. Suraj said he wouldn't play for more than ten minutes, because he had some business to attend to; he kicked off his chappals and ran barefoot after the ball. Everyone was playing barefoot. It was an informal game, and the players were of all ages and sizes, from bearded Sikhs to small boys of six or seven. Suraj ran all over the place without actually getting in touch with the ball — he wasn't much good at football — and finally got into a scramble before the goal, fell and scratched his knee. He retired from the game even sooner than he had intended.

The scratch wasn't bad but there was some blood on

237

his knee. He wiped it clean with his handkerchief and limped off the maidaan. He went in the direction of the railway station, but not through the bazaar. He went by way of the canal, which came from the foot of the nearest mountain, flowed through the town and down to the river. Beside the canal were the washerwomen, scrubbing and beating out clothes on the stone banks.

The canal was only a metre wide but, due to recent rain, the current was swift and noisy. Suraj stood on the bank, watching the rush of water. There was an inlet at one place, and here some children were bathing, and some were rushing up and down the bank, wearing nothing at all, shouting to each other in high spirits. Suraj felt like taking a dip too, but he did not know any of the children here; most of them were from very poor families. Hands in pockets, he walked along the canal banks.

The sun had risen and was pouring through the branches of the trees that lined the road. The leaves made shadowy patterns on the ground. Suraj tried hard not to think of his school report, but he knew that at any moment now the postman would be handing over a long brown envelope to his mother. He tried to imagine his mother's expression when she read the report; but the more he tried to picture her face, the more certain he was that, on knowing his result, she would show no expression at all. And having no expression on her face was much worse than having one.

Suraj heard the whistle of a train, and knew he was not far from the station. He cut through a field, climbed a hillock and ran down the slope until he was near the railway tracks. Here came the train, screeching and puffing: in the distance, a big black beetle, and then, when the carriages swung into sight, a centipede ...

Suraj stood a good twenty metres away from the lines, on the slope of the hill. As the train passed, he pulled the handkerchief off his knee and began to wave it furiously. There was something about passing trains that filled him with awe and excitement. All those passengers, with mysterious lives and mysterious destinations, were people he wanted to know, people whose mysteries he wanted to unfold. He had been in a train recently, when his parents had taken him to bathe in the sacred river, Ganga, at Hardwar. He wished he could be in a train now; or, better still, be an engine-driver, with no more books and teachers and school reports. He did not know of any thirteen-year-old engine-drivers, but he saw himself driving the engine, shouting orders to the stoker; it made him feel powerful to be in control of a mighty steam-engine.

Someone — another boy — returned his wave, and the two waved at each other for a few seconds, and then the train had passed, its smoke spiralling backwards.

Suraj felt a little lonely now. Somehow, the passing of the train left him with a feeling of being alone in a wide empty world. He was feeling hungry too. He went back to the field where he had seen some lichi trees, climbed into one of them and began plucking and peeling and eating the juicy red-skinned fruit. No one seemed to own the lichi trees because, although a dog appeared below and began barking, no one else appeared. Suraj kept spitting lichi seeds at the dog, and the dog kept barking at him. Eventually the dog lost interest and slunk off.

Suraj began to feel drowsy in the afternoon heat. The lichi trees offered a lot of shade below, so he came down from the tree and sat on the grass, his back resting against the tree-trunk. A mynah-bird came hopping up to his feet and looked at him curiously, its head to one side.

Insects kept buzzing around Suraj. He swiped at them once or twice, but then couldn't make the effort to keep swiping. He opened his shirt buttons. The air was very hot, very still; the only sound was the faint buzzing of the insects. His head fell forward on his chest.

He opened his eyes to find himself being shaken, and looked up into the round, cheerful face of his friend Ranji.

"What are you doing, sleeping here?" asked Ranji, who was a couple of years younger than Suraj. "Have you run away from home?"

"Not yet," said Suraj. "And what are *you* doing here?"

"Came for lichis."

"So did I."

They sat together for a while and talked and ate lichis. Then Ranji suggested that they visit the bazaar to eat fried pakoras.

"I haven't any money," said Suraj.

"That doesn't matter," said Ranji, who always seemed to be in funds. "I have two rupees."

So they walked to the bazaar. They crossed the field, walked back past the canal, skirted the maidaan, came to the clock tower and entered the bazaar.

The evening crowd had just begun to fill the road, and there was a lot of bustle and noise: the street-vendors called their wares in high, strident voices; children shouted and women bargained. There was a medley of smells and aromas coming from the little restaurants and sweet shops, and a medley of colour in the bangle and kite shops. Suraj and Ranji ate their pakoras, felt thirsty, and gazed at the rows and rows of coloured bottles at the cold-drinks shop, where at least ten varieties of sweet, sticky, fizzy drinks were available. But they had already finished the two rupees, so there was nothing for them to do but quench their thirst at the municipal tap.

Afterwards they wandered down the crowded street, examining the shop-fronts, commenting on the passers-by, and every now and then greeting some friend or acquaintance. Darkness came on suddenly, and then the bazaar was lit up, the big shops with bright electric and neon lights, the street-vendors with oil-lamps. The bazaar at night was even more exciting than during the day.

They traversed the bazaar from end to end, and when they were at the clock tower again, Ranji said he had to go home, and left Suraj. It was nearing Suraj's dinner-time and so, unwillingly, he too turned homewards. He did not want it to appear that he was deliberately staying out late because of the school report.

The lights were on in the front room when he got home. He waited outside, secure in the darkness of the veran-dah, watching the lighted room. His mother would be waiting for him, she would probably have the report in her hand or on the kitchen shelf, and she would have lots and lots of questions to ask him.

241

All the cares of the world seemed to descend on Suraj as he crept into the house.

"You're late," said his mother. "Come and have your food."

Suraj said nothing, but removed his shoes outside the kitchen and sat down cross-legged on the kitchen floor, which was where he took his meals. He was tired and hungry. He no longer cared about anything.

"One of your class-fellows dropped in," said his mother. "He said your reports were sent out today. They'll arrive tomorrow."

Tomorrow! Suraj felt a great surge of relief.

But then, just as suddenly, his spirits fell again.

Tomorrow ... a further postponement of the dreaded moment, another night and another morning ... something would have to be done about it!

"Ma," he said abruptly. "Somi has asked me to his house again tomorrow."

"I don't know how his mother puts up with you so often," said Suraj's mother.

Suraj lay awake in bed, planning the morrow's activities: a game of cricket or football on the maidaan; perhaps a dip in the canal; a half-hour watching the trains thunder past; and in the evening an hour in the bazaar, among the kites and balloons and rose-coloured fizzy drinks and round dripping syrupy sweets ... Perhaps, in the morning, he could persuade his mother to give him two or three rupees ... It would be his last rupees for quite some time.

When the Guavas are Ripe

Guava trees are easy to climb. And guavas are good to eat. So it's little wonder that an orchard of guava trees is a popular place with boys and girls.

Just across the road from Ranji's house, on the other side of a low wall, was a large guava orchard. The monsoon rains were almost over. It was a warm humid day in September, and the guavas were ripening, turning from green to gold; no longer hard, but growing soft and sweet and juicy.

The schools were closed because of a religious festival. Ranji's father was at work in his office. Ranji's mother was enjoying an afternoon siesta on a cot in the backyard. His grandmother was busy teaching her pet parrot to recite a prayer.

"I feel like getting into those guava trees," said Ranji to himself. "It's months since I climbed a tree."

He was soon across the road and over the wall and into the trees. He chose a tree that grew in the middle of the orchard, where it was unlikely that he would be disturbed; then he climbed swiftly into its branches. A cluster of guavas swung just above him. He reached up for one of them, but to his surprise he found himself clutching a small bare foot which had suddenly been thrust through the foliage.

Having caught the foot, Ranji did not let go. Instead he pulled hard on it. There was a squeal and someone came toppling down on him. Ranji found himself clutching at arms and legs. Together they crashed through a couple of branches and landed with a thud on the soft ground beneath the tree.

Ranji and the intruder struggled fiercely. They rolled about on the grass. Ranji tried a judo hold — without any success. Then he saw that his opponent was a girl. It was his friend and neighbour, Koki.

"It's you!" he gasped.

"It's me," said Koki. "And what are *you* doing here?"

"Get your knee out of my stomach and I'll tell you."

When he had recovered his breath, he said, "I just felt like climbing a tree."

"So did I."

He stared at her. There was guava juice at the corners of her mouth and on her chin.

"Are the guavas good?" he asked.

"Quite sweet, in this tree," said Koki. "You find another tree for yourself, Ranji. There must be thirty or forty trees to choose from."

"And all going to waste," said Ranji. "Look, some of the guavas have been spoilt by the birds."

"Nobody wants them, it seems."

Koki climbed back into her tree, and Ranji obligingly

walked a little further and climbed another tree. After a few polite exchanges they fell silent, their attention given over entirely to the eating of guavas.

"I've eaten five," said Koki after some time.

"You'd better stop."

"You're only saying that because you've just started."

"Well, three's enough for me."

"I'm getting a tummy-ache, I think."

"I warned you. Come on, I'll take you home. We can come back tomorrow. There are still lots of guavas left. Hundreds!"

"I don't think I want to eat any more," said Koki.

She felt better the next day — so well, in fact, that Ranji found her leaning on the gate, waiting for him to join her. She was accompanied by her small brother, Teju, who was only six and very mischievous.

"How are you feeling today?" asked Ranji.

"Hungry," said Koki.

"Why did you bring your brother?"

"He wants to start climbing trees."

Soon they were in the orchard. Ranji and Koki helped Teju into the branches of one of the smaller trees and then made for other trees, disturbing a party of parrots who flew in circles round the orchard, screaming their protests.

Two boys and a girl talking to each other from three different trees can make quite a lot of noise, and it wasn't only the birds who were disturbed. Though they did not know it, the orchard belonged to a wealthy property-dealer and he employed a watchman, whose duty it was to keep away birds, children, monkeys, flying-foxes and other fruit-eating pests. But on a hot sultry afternoon Gopal the watchman could not resist taking a nap. He was stretched out under a shady jack-fruit tree, snoring so loudly that the flies who had been buzzing round him felt that a storm was brewing and kept their distance.

He woke to the sound of voices raised high in glee. Sitting up, he brushed a ladybird from his long moustache, then seized his lathi, a long stout stick usually carried by watchmen.

"Who's there?" he shouted, struggling to his feet.

There was a sudden silence in the trees.

"Who's there?" he called again.

No answer.

"I must have been dreaming," he muttered, and was preparing to lie down and take another nap when Teju, who had been watching him, burst into laughter.

"Ho!" shouted the watchman, coming to life again. "Thieves! I'll settle you!" And he began striding towards the centre of the orchard, boasting all the time of his physical prowess. "I'm not afraid of thieves, bandits, or wild beasts! I'll have you know that I was once the wrestling champion of the entire district of Dehra. Come on out and fight me if you dare!"

"Run!" hissed Koki, scrambling down from her tree.

"Run!" shouted Ranji, as though it were a cricket match.

Teju was so startled by the sudden activity that he tumbled out of his tree and began crying, and Ranji and Koki

had to go to his aid.

The sight of an enormous ex-wrestler bearing down on them was enough to make Teju stop crying and get to his feet. Then all three were fleeing across the grove, the watchman a little way behind them, waving his lathi and shouting at the top of his voice. Although he was an ex-wrestler (or perhaps because of it) he could not run very fast, and was still huffing and puffing some twenty metres behind them when they climbed up and over the wall. He could not climb walls either.

They ran off in different directions before returning home.

Next day, Ranji met Koki and Teju at the far end of the road.

"Is he there?" asked Koki.

"I haven't seen him. But he must be around somewhere."

"Maybe he's gone for his lunch. We'll just walk past and take a quick look."

The three of them strolled casually down the road. Koki said the gardens were looking very pretty. Teju gazed admiringly at a boy flying a kite from a roof-top. Ranji kept one eye on the road and one eye on the orchard wall. A squirrel ran along the top of the wall; the parrots were back in the guava trees.

They moved closer to the wall. Ranji leaned casually against it and Koki began to pick little daisies growing at the edge of the road. Teju, unable to hide his curiosity, pulled himself up on the wall and looked over. At the

248

same time, Gopal the watchman, who had been hiding behind the wall waiting for them, stood up slowly and glared fiercely at Teju.

Teju gulped, but he did not flinch. He was looking straight into the watchman's red angry eyes.

"And what can I do for you?" growled Gopal.

"I was just looking," said Teju.

"At what?"

"At the view."

Gopal was a little baffled. They looked just like the children he'd chased away yesterday, but he couldn't be sure. They didn't *look* guilty. But did children ever look guilty?

"There's a better view from the other side of the road," he said gruffly. "Now be off!"

"What lovely guavas," said Koki, smiling sweetly. There weren't many people who could resist that smile!

"True," said Ranji, with the air of one who was an expert on guavas and all things good to eat. "They are just the right size and colour. I don't think I've seen better. But they'll be spoilt by the birds if you don't gather them soon."

"It's none of your business," said the watchman.

"Just look at his muscles," said Teju, trying a different approach. "He's really strong!"

Gopal looked pleased for once. He was proud of his former prowess, even though he was now rather flabby around the waist.

"You look like a wrestler," said Ranji.

"*I am* a wrestler," said Gopal.

"I told you so," said Koki. "What else could he be?"

"I'm a retired wrestler," said Gopal.

"You don't look retired," said Teju, fast learning that flattery can get you almost anywhere.

Gopal swelled with pride; such admiration hadn't come his way for a long time. To Koki he looked like a bull-frog swelling up, but she thought it better not to say so.

"Do you want to see my muscles?" he asked.

"Yes, yes!" they cried. "Do show us!"

Gopal peeled off his shirt and thumped his chest. It sounded like a drum. They were really impressed. Then he bent his elbow and his biceps stood up like cricket balls.

"You can touch them," he said generously.

Teju poked a finger into Gopal's biceps.

"Mister Universe!" he exclaimed.

Gopal glowed all over. He liked these children. How intelligent they were! Not everyone had the sense to appreciate his strength, his manliness, his magnificent physique!

"Climb over the wall and join me," he said. "Come sit on the grass and I'll tell you about the time when I was a wrestling champion."

Over the wall they came, and sat politely on the grass. Gopal told them about some of his exploits; how he had vanquished a world-famous wrestler in five seconds flat, and how he had saved a carload of travellers from drowning by single-handedly dragging their car out of a river. They listened patiently. Then Teju mentioned that he

250

was feeling hungry.

"Hungry?" said Gopal. "Why didn't you tell me before? I'll bring you some guavas, that's all there is to eat here. I know which tree has the best ones. And they're all going to rot if no one eats them — no one's buying the crop this year, the owner's price is too high!"

Gopal hurried off and soon returned with a basket full of guavas.

"Help yourselves," he said. "But don't eat too many, you'll get sick."

So they munched guavas and listened to Gopal tell them about the time he was waylaid by three bandits and how he threw them all into the village pond.

"Will you come again tomorrow?" asked Gopal eagerly, when the guavas were finished and the children got up to leave. "Come tomorrow and I'll tell you another story."

"We'll come tomorrow," said Teju, looking at all the guava trees still laden with fruit.

Somehow it seemed very important to Gopal that they should come again. It was lonely in the orchard. Koki sensed this, and said, "We like your stories."

"They are good stories," said Ranji, even if they were not entirely true, he thought ...

They climbed over the wall and waved goodbye to Gopal.

They came again the next day.

And even when the guava season was over and Gopal had nothing to offer them but his stories, they went to see him because by that time they had grown to like him.

251

The King and the Tree-Goddess

This is one of the stories Koki's grandmother told the children on a wet monsoon evening, when it was impossible to play outside. Grandmother loved trees, and this was one of her favourite tree stories.

There was once a king living in the Himalayan foothills, who longed to build himself a palace more beautiful than any he had seen in that part of the world. He could not make it richer, taller or stronger than any other without going to a great deal of expense and trouble. So he decided to build something different: the entire palace was to be supported by one column only, and that column was to be made from the tallest tree in the kingdom.

In the Himalayas there are many tall trees — spruce and pine, oak and deodar. And the tallest and the strongest are the deodars, whose very name, *Deo-Dar*, means Tree of God.

The King sent for his Prime Minister and said, "Send men to my forests far and near, and tell them to cut down and bring to this city without delay the largest deodar they can find."

"But the deodar is a sacred tree," protested his daughter. "It is used only for building temples."

"All the more reason for me to have one," said the King. "My palace shall be as magnificent as any temple!"

The Prime Minister sent out thirty men but they soon returned, saying that though there were many great deodars in the kingdom, they could never carry or drag them over so much difficult country as lay between the forests and the city.

When the King heard this, he called his son and said, "Take your horsemen, and with the help of your horses, bring me one of these trees."

The prince rode out with his horsemen but returned after a few days, saying, "No horses could move such a tree an inch. We have tried oxen too, but without any success."

"Well, then, try elephants," said the King.

Elephants were brought from the plains, but the hills were too steep for them, and the paths too narrow; they had to return to the valley.

"Very well," said the King angrily. "In one of my own parks you must find me a tree just as big as any in the forests. Bring it to me within seven days."

After much searching, the King's men found a splendid deodar tree growing not far from the city. It was worshipped by the people of many villages round about, because within it lived a Goddess, and it was she who gave to the tree its great strength, size and beauty.

When the Prime Minister and his men had decided

that the column for the King's palace must be made from this lofty deodar tree, they came with garlands, lamps and music to pay their respects to the Goddess inside, and to warn her that she must leave her abode. Within seven days it had to be cut to the ground.

They lit their lamps and placed them in a circle round the tree. They hung their garlands upon the branches and tied nosegays among the leaves. Then, joining hands, some danced, and others sang:

> With cruel axe we've come
> To fell your age-long home;
> Forgive us, great Tree-Goddess —
> We dance before your throne!
> To please the King must we
> Cut down your loveliest tree.

The Tree-Goddess heard, and understood what was about to happen. She remained quiet as a resting breeze for a few moments, and then all her leaves began to whisper and her topmost branches bowed. The men went away satisfied that she had heard and understood.

That night, when the King was asleep, a glorious figure draped in shining green foliage appeared to him, and spoke in a voice that was like the rustle of autumn leaves:

"I am the Goddess of the Deodar tree, great King. Your men have told me that you intend to cut me down. I have come to beg you to change your mind."

"No, my mind is made up," answered the King in his dream. "Yours is the only tree in all my parks strong enough to support by itself a palace, and therefore I must have it."

"But consider, oh King! For hundreds of years I have been worshipped by the people of all the villages in your kingdom, and nothing but good has gone out from me to them. The birds nest in me. I send a most lovely shade upon the grass. Men rest against my trunk and wild creatures rub themselves against me. The earth blesses me, and sends up new plants and herbs under my protective arms. I bind the earth with my strong roots. Children play at my feet, and women returning from the fields seek refuge in my coolness."

"All true enough, good Tree-Goddess," said the King, "but all the same I cannot spare you. My mind is made up, my will cannot be shaken."

The Tree-Goddess sank her head upon her breast and spoke in tones of great sorrow:

"Then, mighty King, grant me one last request. Let me be felled in three parts. First my head, with its crown of waving greenery. Next my middle, with its hundred strong arms and hands. And last my base, which bears the heaviest and knottiest of my limbs upon it."

"This is a strange request," said the King. "I have never before heard of someone who wished to suffer the death stroke *thrice!* Why not suffer it once, and have done with it?"

"The reason is plain," said the Tree-Goddess. "Dozens of young deodar trees have sprung from me, and have grown up around me. Should you fell me with one mighty stroke, my weight would certainly crush all my children to death. But if I suffer the stroke three times, and fall in three pieces, some of the young ones may escape. Is my prayer granted?"

"Indeed it is," said the astonished King, as the Tree-Goddess faded from his vision.

The next morning the King called his children and his ministers and his foresters to him, and told them that he had changed his mind, and that the column for the new palace should be built of stone, not wood.

"For," said he, "within the deodar tree lives a spirit nobler than my own." And he told them of his vision, and they all marvelled.

And the King built his palace upon a great column of stone, and around its base he created a beautiful park, and the children of the city and the surrounding villages flocked to the gardens to sit on the grass and enjoy the many beautiful flowers and trees that had been planted on all sides.

Taking the example of the King, no one built their houses of wood any more. The houses were made of stone, and the great deodars were able to spread freely through the forests.

"And if you go up into the mountains," said Grandmother, "you can still see those forests, all the way up the sacred river Ganga, to its source near the eternal snows."

The Fight

Anil had been less than a month in Dehra when he discovered the pool in the forest. It was the height of summer, and the school he was to join had not yet opened. Having as yet made no friends in the small town in the foothills, he wandered about a good deal by himself, into the hills and forests that stretched away on all sides of the town.

It was hot, very hot, at that time of the year, and Anil, aged thirteen, walked about in his vest and shorts, his brown feet white with the chalky dust that flew up from the ground. The earth was parched, the grass brown, the trees listless, hardly stirring, waiting for a cool wind or a refreshing shower of rain. It was on one of these tiresome days that Anil found the pool in the forest. The water had a gentle green translucency, and he could see the smooth round pebbles at the bottom of the pool. It was fed by a small stream that emerged from a cluster of rocks.

During the monsoon this stream would be a rushing torrent, cascading down from the hills; but during the summer it was barely a trickle. The rocks, however, held the water in the pool, and it didn't dry up like the pools in the plains.

When Anil saw the pool, he didn't hesitate to get into it. He had often been swimming, alone or with friends, when he had lived with his parents in a thirsty town in the middle of the Rajasthan desert. There, he had known only sticky, muddy pools, where buffaloes wallowed in the slush. He had never seen a pool like this — so clean and cool and inviting. He threw off all his clothes, as he had always done when swimming in the plains, and leapt into the water. His limbs were supple, and his dark body glistened in patches of sunlit water.

The next day he came again to quench his body in the cool waters of the forest pool. He was there for almost an hour, sliding in and out of the limpid green water, or lying stretched out on the smooth yellow rocks in the shade of broad-leaved sal trees.

It was while he lay naked on a rock that he noticed another boy standing a little distance away, staring at him in a rather hostile manner. The other boy was a year or two older than Anil, taller and thick-set, with a broad nose. He had only just noticed Anil, and he stood at the edge of the pool, wearing a pair of bathing shorts, waiting for Anil to explain himself.

When Anil didn't say anything, the other called out. "What are you doing here, mister?"

Anil, who was prepared to be friendly, was surprised at the other's hostility.

"I am swimming," he replied. "Why don't you join me?"

258

"I always swim alone," said the other. "This is my pool. I did not invite you to it. And why aren't you wearing any clothes?"

"It is not your business what I wear or do not wear. I have nothing to be ashamed of."

"You skinny fellow, put on your clothes!"

"Fat fool, take yours off!"

This was too much for the stranger. He strode up to Anil, who still sat on the rock; and, planting his broad feet firmly on the sand, said (as though it would settle the matter once and for all), "Don't you know I am a Punjabi? I do not take insults from villagers like you!"

"So you like to fight with villagers," said Anil. "Well, I do not belong to your village. I am a Rajput!"

"I am a Punjabi!"

"I am a Rajput!"

They had reached an impasse. One had said he was a Punjabi, the other had proclaimed himself a Rajput. There was little else that could be said.

"You understand that I am a Punjabi?" repeated the stranger, uneasily aware that the other had not seemed sufficiently impressed.

"I have heard you say it three times," replied Anil.

"Then why don't you run off?"

"I am waiting for you to run!"

"I shall have to thrash you," said the Punjabi boy, assuming a violent attitude and showing Anil the palm of his hand.

"Let me see you do it," said Anil.

"You *will* see me do it," said the Punjabi boy.

Anil waited. The other boy made an odd, hissing sound. They stared each other in the eye for almost a minute. Then the Punjabi boy slapped Anil across the face with all his strength. Anil staggered back, feeling giddy. There were thick red finger-marks on his cheek.

"There you are," exclaimed his assailant. "Will you be off now?"

By way of reply, Anil swung his arm up and pushed a hard, bony fist into his adversary's face.

And then they were at each other's throats, swaying together on the rock, tumbling on to the sand, rolling over and over, their arms and legs locked in a fierce struggle. Clawing, grasping and cursing, they rolled right into the shallows of the pool.

Even in the water they continued fighting. Spluttering and covered with mud, they groped for each other's heads and throats. But after five minutes of frenzied struggle, neither boy had emerged victorious. Their bodies heaving with exhaustion, they stood back from each other, making tremendous efforts to speak.

"Now — now do you realise — I am a Punjabi?" gasped the stranger.

"Do you — know I am a Rajput?" said Anil with difficulty.

They gave a moment's consideration to each other's answers, and in that moment of silence there was only their heavy breathing and the rapid pounding of their hearts.

"Then you will not leave the pool?" said the Punjabi boy.

"I will not leave it," said Anil.

"Then we shall have to continue the fight," said the other.

"All right," said Anil.

But neither boy moved, neither took the initiative.

Then the Punjabi boy had an inspiration.

"We will continue the fight tomorrow," he said. "If you dare to come back tomorrow, we will continue the fight, and I will not let you off as easily as I have done today!"

"I will come tomorrow," said Anil. "I will be ready for you."

They turned their backs on each other and returned to their respective rocks, where they gathered their belongings, then left the forest by different routes.

When Anil got home, he found it difficult to account for the cuts and bruises that showed on his face, arms and legs. He could not conceal the fact that he had been in a bad fight, and his mother insisted on his staying at home for the rest of the day.

That evening, though, he slipped out of the house and went to the bazaar where he found comfort and solace in a bottle of vividly coloured lemonade and a banana-leaf full of hot, sweet jalebis. He had just finished the lemonade when he saw his recent adversary coming down the road.

Anil's first impulse was to turn away and look elsewhere; his second to throw the empty bottle at his enemy; but he did neither of these things. Instead, he stood his ground and scowled at his opponent. And the Punjabi boy said nothing either, but scowled back with equal ferocity.

The next day was as hot as the previous one. Anil felt weak and lazy and not at all eager for a fight. His body was stiff and sore after the previous day's encounter. But he couldn't refuse the challenge. Not to turn up at the pool would be an acknowledgement of defeat. But from the way he was feeling, he knew he would be beaten in another fight. Yet he must defy his enemy, outwit him if possible. To surrender now would be to forfeit all rights to the pool in the forest; and he knew it was his pool.

He was half-hoping that the Punjabi boy would have forgotten the challenge, but as soon as Anil arrived he saw his opponent stripped to the waist, sitting on a rock at the far end of the pool. The Punjabi boy was rubbing oil on his body, massaging it into his broad thighs. He saw Anil beneath the sal trees, and called a challenge across the water.

"Come over to this side and fight!" he shouted.

But Anil was not going to submit to any conditions laid down by his opponent.

"Come *this* side and fight," he shouted back defiantly.

"Swim over and fight me here!" called the other. "Or perhaps you cannot swim the length of this pool!"

Anil could have swum the length of the pool a dozen times without tiring, and in this department he knew he could show the Punjabi boy his superiority. Slipping out of his vest and shorts, he dived straight into the water, cutting through it like a golden fish and surfacing with hardly a splash. The Punjabi boy's mouth hung open in amazement.

"You can dive!" he exclaimed.

"It is easy," said Anil, treading water and waiting for another challenge. "Can't you dive?"

"No," said the other. "I jump straight in. But if you will tell me how, I'll make a dive."

"It is easy," said Anil. "Stand straight on the rock, hold your arms out, and allow your head to displace your feet."

The Punjabi boy stood up, stiff and straight, stretched out his arms, and threw himself at the water. He landed flat on his belly, with a crash that sent the birds screaming out of the trees.

Anil burst into laughter.

"Are you trying to empty the pool?" he asked, as the Punjabi boy came to the surface, spouting water like a small whale.

"Wasn't it good?" asked the boy, evidently proud of his feat.

"Not very good," said Anil. "You should have more practice. See, I will do it again!"

And pulling himself up on a rock, he executed another perfect dive. The Punjabi boy waited for him to come up, but, swimming under water in a world of soft lights and crooked sunshine, Anil circled the boy and came up from behind.

"How did you do that?" asked the astonished youth.

"Can't you swim under water?" asked Anil.

"No, but I will try."

The Punjabi boy made a tremendous effort to plunge to the bottom of the pool; indeed, he thought he had gone right down, but his bottom, like a duck's, remained above the surface.

Anil, however, did not want to sound too discouraging. He was involved in a game of high diplomacy.

"That was not bad," he said. "But you need a lot of practice."

"Will you teach me?" asked his enemy.

"If you like, I will teach you."

"You must teach me. If you do not teach me, I will thrash you. Will you come here every day and teach me?"

"If you like," said Anil. They had pulled themselves out of the water and were sitting side by side on a smooth grey rock.

"My name is Vijay," said the Punjabi boy. "What is yours?"

"It is Anil."

"I am strong, am I not?" said Vijay, bending his arm so that a ball of muscle stood up.

"You are strong," said Anil. "You are like a wrestler, a pahlwan."

"One day I will be Mister Universe!" said Vijay, slapping his thighs, which shook with the impact of his hand.

He looked critically at Anil's hard, thin body. "You are quite strong yourself," he conceded, "but you are too bony. I know, you people do not eat enough. You must come and have your meals with me. I drink a pitcher of milk every day. You see, we have got our own cow. Be my friend, and I will make you a real pahlwan like me! I know — if you teach me to dive and swim under water, I will make you a pahlwan. This is fair, isn't it?"

"It's fair," said Anil, though he doubted if he was getting the better of the exchange.

Vijay put his arm around the younger boy's shoulders and said, "We are friends now, yes?"

They looked at each other with unflinching eyes, and in that moment a friendship was born.

"We are friends," said Anil.

The birds had settled again in the branches of the sal trees, and the pool was still and limpid in the afternoon shadows.

"It is our pool," said Vijay. "Nobody else can come here. Who would dare?"

"Yes, who would dare?" said Anil, smiling with the knowledge that he had won the day.

The Window

When Amir was thirteen, he decided that he was old enough to have a room of his own.

"What for?" asked his mother.

"The kids make too much noise," he said, referring to his younger brothers and sisters. "I can't study."

"Well, if you really want to study, you can have your own room," said his grandfather, who owned the old building. "There's the room on the roof."

So Amir took the room on the roof.

It was a long, low building with large cracks in the walls from which peepul trees were growing. Amir's grandfather said he couldn't afford to have it repaired. There were a number of tenants in the building and they were paying rents that had been fixed forty years back, when rents were very low, so there wasn't much money coming in. Amir's father had a tailor's shop in the bazaar, but that didn't make much money either. The building had a flat roof, with just the one small room — called a barsati — opening on to it. From the window of his room Amir looked out upon a world quite different from the world below.

The banyan tree, just opposite, was his, and its inhabitants his subjects. There were two squirrels, several mynahs, a crow and, at night, a pair of flying foxes. The squirrels were busy in the afternoon, the birds in the morning and evening, the foxes at night. Amir wasn't very busy. He'd look at his books now and then, but decided that it wasn't a very good year for studying. There was much more to learn from looking out of his window.

At first he felt lonely in the room. But then he discovered the power of the window. It looked out on the banyan tree and the mango grove, on the rather untidy garden, on the broad path running past the building, and out over the roofs of other houses, over roads and fields, as far as the horizon. The path was a busy one: fruit and vegetable vendors came and went, as did the toy-seller and the balloon-man, their wares strung on poles; there were boys on cycles, babies in prams, schoolgirls chattering, housewives quarrelling, old men gossiping ... all passed his way, the way of his window.

Early that summer a tonga came rattling and jingling down the path and stopped in front of the building. A girl and an elderly lady got down, while a servant unloaded their luggage. They went into the house and the tonga moved off.

The next day the girl looked up from the garden and saw Amir at the window.

She had black hair that came to her shoulders. Her eyes were black, like her hair, and just as shiny. She must have been about eleven years old.

268

"Hallo," said Amir.

She looked up at him suspiciously. "Who are you?" she asked.

"I am a ghost."

She laughed, and her laugh had a gay, mocking quality: "You look like one!"

Amir didn't think her remark was very funny, but he had asked for it.

"What are you doing up there?" she asked.

"Practising magic," he said.

She laughed again but this time without the mockery. "I don't believe you," she said.

"Why don't you come up and see for yourself?"

She came round to the steps and began climbing them slowly, cautiously. When she entered the room, she stared at Amir and said: "Where's your magic?"

"Come here," he said, and he took her to the window and showed her his world.

She said nothing, just stared out of the window. Then she turned and smiled at Amir, and they were friends.

He only knew that she was called Chummo, and that she had come with her aunt for the summer months. He did not need to know any more about her, and she did not need to know any more about him except that he wasn't really a ghost.

She came up the steps nearly every day and joined Amir at the window. There was a lot of excitement to be had in the world of the window, especially when the monsoon rains arrived.

At the first rumblings, women would rush outside to

269

retrieve their washing from the clothes-line and, if there was a breeze, to chase a few garments across the compound. When the rain came, it came with a vengeance, making a bog of the garden and a river of the path.

A cyclist would come riding furiously down the path, an elderly gentleman would be having difficulty with his umbrella, naked toddlers would be frisking about in the rain. Sometimes Amir would run out on the roof and shout and dance in the rain. And the rain would come through the open door and window of the room, flooding the floor and making an island of the bed.

But the window was more fun than anything else.

"It's like a film," said Chummo. "The window is the screen, the world outside is the picture."

Soon the mangoes were ripe and Chummo was in the branches of the mango tree as often as she was at Amir's window. Amir was supposed to be deep in study, so any forays into the mango tree on his part would not have pleased his grandfather. But from the window he had a good view of the tree, and he could speak to Chummo from about the same level. She brought him unripe mangoes, and they ate far too many of them and had tummy aches for the rest of the day.

"Let's make a garden on the roof," said Chummo.

"How do we do that?" asked Amir.

"It's easy. We bring up mud and bricks and make the flower-beds. Then we plant the seeds. We'll grow all sorts of flowers."

"The roof will fall in," said Amir.

"Never mind," said Chummo.

270

They spent two days carrying buckets of mud up the steps to the roof and laying out the flower-beds. It was hard work, but Chummo did most of it. When the beds were ready, they had a planting ceremony. But apart from a few small plants collected from the garden below, they had only one kind of seed — pumpkin.

"I can't eat pumpkins," said Amir.

"Have you ever met anyone who likes pumpkins?" asked Chummo.

"No. Everyone hates them."

"True. And yet people keep on growing them, and selling them, and forcing children to eat them."

"They just do it to make us suffer," said Amir.

"True. We'll present our pumpkins to our enemies."

So they planted the pumpkin seeds in the mud and felt proud of themselves.

But the following night it rained very heavily, and in the morning they discovered that everything — except the bricks — had been washed away.

So they returned to the window.

A mynah had been in a fight and the feathers had been knocked off its head. A bougainvillaea creeper that had been climbing the wall had sent a long green shoot in through the window.

Chummo said, "Now we can't shut the window without spoiling the creeper."

"Then we won't close the window," said Amir.

And they let the creeper into the room.

The rains passed and an autumn wind came whispering through the branches of the banyan tree. There were red leaves on the ground and the wind picked them up and blew them about so that they looked like butterflies. Amir would watch the sunrise, the sky all red until the first rays splashed the window-sill and crept up the walls of the room. And in the evening Chummo and Amir would watch the sun go down in a sea of fluffy clouds. Sometimes the clouds were pink, sometimes orange; they were nearly always coloured clouds, framed in the window.

"I'm going tomorrow," said Chummo one evening.

Amir was too surprised to say anything.

"You stay here all the time, don't you?" she said.

Amir nodded.

"When I come again next year, you'll still be here, won't you?"

"I suppose so," said Amir.

In the morning the tonga was at the door, and the servant, the aunt and Chummo were in it. Amir was at his window, Chummo waved up to him. Then the driver flicked the pony's reins, the tonga creaked and rattled, the bell jingled. Down the path and through the compound gate went the tonga, and all the time Chummo waved.

When the tonga was out of sight, Amir took the spray of bougainvillaea and pushed it out of the room. Then he closed the window. It would be opened only when the spring and Chummo came again.

Mukesh Starts a Zoo

On a visit to Delhi with his parents, Mukesh spent two crowded hours at the zoo. He was dazzled by the many colourful birds, fascinated by the reptiles, charmed by the gibbons and chimps, and awestruck by the big cats — the lions, tigers and leopards. There was no zoo in the small town of Dehra where he lived, and the jungle was some way across the river-bed. So, as soon as he got home, he decided that he would have a zoo of his own.

"I'm going to start a zoo," he announced at breakfast, the day after his return.

"But you don't have any birds or animals," said Dolly, his little sister.

"I'll soon find them," said Mukesh. "That's what a zoo is all about — collecting animals."

He was gazing at the whitewashed walls of the verandah, where a gecko, a small wall lizard, was in pursuit of a fly. A little later Mukesh was trying to catch the lizard. But it was more alert than it looked, and always managed to keep a few inches ahead of his grasp.

"That's not the way to catch a lizard," said Teju,

appearing on the verandah steps. Teju and his sister Koki lived next door.

"*You* catch it, then," said Mukesh.

Teju fetched a stick from the garden, where it had been used to prop up sweet-peas. He used the stick to tip the lizard off the wall and into a shoe-box.

"You'll be my Head Keeper," said Mukesh, and soon he and Teju were at work in the back garden, setting up enclosures with a roll of wire-netting they had found in the poultry shed.

"What else can we have in the zoo?" asked Teju. "We need more than a lizard."

"There's your grandmother's parrot," said Mukesh.

"That's a good idea. But we won't tell her about it — not yet. I don't think she'd lend it to us. You see, it's a *religious* parrot. She's taught it lots of prayers and chants."

"Then people are sure to come and listen to it. They'll pay, too."

"We must have the parrot, then. What else?"

"Well, there's my dog," said Mukesh. "He's very fierce."

"But a dog isn't a zoo animal."

"Mine is — he's a *wild* dog. Look, he's black all over and he's got yellow eyes. There's no other dog like him."

Mukesh's dog, who spent most of his time sleeping on the verandah, raised his head and obligingly revealed his yellow eyes.

"He's got jaundice," said Teju.

"They've always been yellow."

"All right, then, we've got a lizard, a parrot and a black

275

dog with yellow eyes."

"Koki has a white rabbit. Will she lend it to us?"

"I don't know. She thinks a lot of her rabbit. Maybe we can *rent* it from her."

"And there's Sitaram's donkey."

Sitaram, the dhobi-boy, usually used a donkey to deliver and collect the laundry from the houses along this particular street.

"Do you really want a donkey?" asked Teju doubtfully.

"Why not? It's a wild donkey. Haven't you heard of them?"

"I've heard of a wild ass, but not a wild donkey."

"Well, they're all related to each other — asses, donkeys and mules."

"Why don't you paint black stripes on it and call it a zebra?"

"No, that's cheating. It's got to be a proper zoo. No tricks — it's not a circus!"

On Saturday afternoon, a large placard with corrected spelling announced the opening of the zoo. It hung from the branches of the jack-fruit tree. Children were allowed in free but grown-ups had to buy tickets at fifty paise each, and Koki and Dolly were selling home-made tickets to the occasional passer-by or parent who happened to look in. Mukesh and his friends had worked hard at making notices for the various enclosures and each resident of the zoo was appropriately named.

The first attraction was a large packing-case filled with an assortment of house-lizards. They looked rather

276

sluggish, having been generously fed with a supply of beetles and other insects.

Then came an enclosure in which Koki's white rabbit was on display. Freshly washed and brushed, it looked very cuddly and was praised by all.

Staring at it with evil intent from behind wire-netting was Mukesh's dog — RARE BLACK DOG WITH YEL-LOW EYES read the notice. Those yellow eyes were now trying hard to hypnotise the pink eyes of Koki's nervous rabbit. The dog pawed at the ground, trying to dig its way out from under the fence to get at the rabbit.

Tethered to a mango tree was a placard saying WILD ASS FROM KUTCH. A distant relative it may have been, but everyone recognised it as the local washerman's beast of burden. Every now and then it tried to break loose, for it was long past its feeding time.

There was also a duck that did not seem to belong to anyone, and a small cow that had strayed in on its own; but the star attraction was the parrot. As it could recite three different prayers, over and over again, it was soon surrounded by a group of admiring parents, all of whom wished they had a parrot who could pray, or rather, do their praying for them. Oddly enough, Koki's grand-mother had chosen that day for visiting the temple, so she was unaware of the fuss that was being made of her pet, or even that it had been made an honorary member of the zoo. Teju had convinced himself she wouldn't mind.

While Mukesh and Teju were escorting visitors around the zoo, lecturing them on wild dogs and wild asses, Koki and Dolly were doing a brisk trade at the ticket counter. They had collected about ten rupees and were hoping for yet more, when there was a disturbance in the enclosures.

The black dog with yellow eyes had finally managed to dig his way out of his cage, and was now busy trying to dig his way *into* the rabbit's compartment. The rabbit was running round and round in panic-stricken circles. Meanwhile, the donkey had finally snapped the rope that held it and, braying loudly, scattered the spectators and made for home.

Koki went to the rescue of her rabbit and soon had it cradled in her arms. The dog now turned his attention to the duck. The duck flew over the packing-case, while the dog landed in it, scattering lizards in all directions.

In all this confusion, no one noticed that the door of the parrot's cage had slipped open. With a squawk and a whirr of wings, the bird shot out of the cage and flew off into a nearby orchard.

"The parrot's gone!" shouted Dolly, and almost immediately a silence fell upon the assembled visitors and children. Even the dog stopped barking. Granny's praying parrot had escaped! How could they possibly face her? Teju wondered if she would believe him if he told her it had flown off to heaven.

"Can anyone see it?" he asked tearfully.

"It's in a mango tree," said Dolly. "It won't come back."

The crowd fell away, unwilling to share any of the blame when Koki's grandmother came home and discovered what had happened.

"What are we going to do now?" asked Teju, looking to Koki for help; but Koki was too upset to suggest anything. Mukesh had an idea.

"I know!" he said. "We'll get another one!"

"How?"

"Well, there's the ten rupees we've collected. We can buy a new parrot for ten rupees!"

"But won't Granny know the difference?" asked Teju.

"All these hill parrots look alike," said Mukesh.

So, taking the cage with them, they hurried off to the bazaar, where they soon found a bird-seller who was happy to sell them a parrot not unlike Granny's. He assured them it would talk.

"It *looks* like your grandmother's parrot," said Mukesh on the way home. "But can it pray?"

"Of course not," said Koki. "But we can teach it."

Koki's grandmother, who was short-sighted, did not notice the substitution; but she complained bitterly that the bird had stopped repeating its prayers and was instead making rude noises and even swearing occasionally.

Teju soon remedied this sad state of affairs.

Every morning he stood in front of the parrot's cage and repeated Granny's prayers. Within a few weeks the bird had learnt to repeat one of them. Granny was happy again — not only because her parrot had started praying once more, but because Teju had started praying too!

The Boy Who Broke the Bank

Nathu, the sweeper-boy, grumbled to himself as he swept the steps of a small local bank, owned for the most part by Seth Govind Ram, a man of wealth whose haphazard business dealings had often brought him to the verge of ruin. Nathu used the small broom hurriedly and carelessly; the dust, after rising in a cloud above his head, settled down again on the steps. As Nathu was banging his pan against a dustbin, Sitaram, the washerman's son, passed by.

Sitaram was on his delivery round. He had a bundle of pressed clothes balanced on his head.

"Don't raise such a dust!" he called out to Nathu. "Are you annoyed because they are still refusing to pay you another five rupees a month?"

"I don't want to talk about it," complained the sweeper-boy. 'I haven't even received my regular pay. And this is the end of the month. Soon two months' pay will be due. Who would think this was a bank, holding up a poor man's salary? As soon as I get my money, I'm off! Not another week will I work in the place."

And Nathu banged his pan against the dustbin two or three times more, just to emphasise his point and give himself confidence.

"Well, I wish you luck," said Sitaram. "I'll be on the look-out for a new job for you." And he plodded barefoot along the road, the big bundle of clothes hiding most of his head and shoulders.

At the fourth house he visited, delivering the washing, Sitaram overheard the woman of the house saying how difficult it was to get someone to sweep the courtyard. Tying up his bundle, Sitaram said: "I know a sweeper-boy who's looking for work. He might be able to work for you from next month. He's with Seth Govind Ram's bank just now, but they are not giving him his pay, and he wants to leave."

"Oh, is that so?" said Mrs Prakash. "And why aren't they paying him?"

"They must be short of money," said Sitaram with a shrug.

Mrs Prakash laughed. "Well, tell him to come and see me when he's free."

Sitaram, glad that he had been of some service both to a friend and to a customer, hoisted his bag on his shoulders and went on his way.

Mrs Prakash had to do some shopping. She gave instructions to her maidservant with regard to the baby and told the cook what she wanted for lunch. Her husband worked for a large company, and they could keep servants and do things in style. Having given her orders, she set out for the bazaar to make her customary tour of the cloth shops.

A large, shady tamarind tree grew near the clock tower, and it was here that Mrs Prakash found her friend, Mrs Bhushan, sheltering from the heat. Mrs Bhushan was fanning herself with a large peacock's feather. She complained that the summer was the hottest in the history of the town. She then showed Mrs Prakash a sample of the cloth she was going to buy, and for five minutes they discussed its shade, texture and design. When they had exhausted the subject, Mrs Prakash said:

"Do you know, my dear, Seth Govind Ram's bank can't even pay its employees. Only this morning I heard a complaint from their sweeper-boy, who hasn't received his pay for two months!"

"It's disgraceful!" exclaimed Mrs Bhushan. "If they can't pay their sweeper, they must be in a bad way. None of the others can be getting paid either."

She left Mrs Prakash at the tamarind tree and went in search of her husband, who was found sitting under the fan in Jugal Kishore's electrical goods shop, playing cards with the owner.

"So there you are!" cried Mrs Bhushan. "I've been looking for you for nearly an hour. Where did you disappear to?"

"Nowhere," replied Mr Bhushan. "Had you remained stationary in one shop, you might have found me. But you go from one to another, like a bee in a flower-garden."

"Now don't start grumbling. The heat is bad enough. I don't know what's happening to this town. Even the

282

bank is going bankrupt."

"What did you say?" said Mr Jugal Kishore, sitting up suddenly. "Which bank?"

"Why, Seth Govind Ram's bank, of course. I hear they've stopped paying their employees — no salary for over three months! Don't tell me you have an account with them, Mr Kishore?"

"No, but my neighbour has!" he said, and he called out to the keeper of the barber shop next door: "Faiz Hussain, have you heard the latest? Seth Govind Ram's bank is about to collapse! You'd better take your money out while there's still time."

Faiz Hussain, who was cutting the hair of an elderly gentleman, was so startled that his hand shook and he nicked his customer's ear. The customer yelped with pain and distresss: pain, because of the cut, and distress, because of the awful news he had just heard. With one side of his neck still unshorn, he leapt out of his chair and sped across the road to a general merchant's store, where there was a telephone. He dialled Seth Govind Ram's number. The Seth was not at home. Where was he, then? The Seth was holidaying in Kashmir. Oh, was *that* so? The elderly gentleman did not believe it. He hurried back to the barber shop and told Faiz Hussain: "The bird has flown! Seth Govind Ram has left town. Definitely, it means a collapse. I'll have the rest of my haircut another time." And he dashed out of the shop and made a bee-line for his office and cheque book.

The news spread through the bazaar with the rapidity of a forest fire. From the general merchant's it travelled to the tea-shop, circulated amongst the customers, and then spread with them in various directions, to the paan-seller, the tailor, the fruit-vendor, the jeweller, the beggar sitting on the pavement ...

Old Ganpat, the beggar, had a crooked leg and had been squatting on the pavement for years, calling for alms. In the evening someone would come with a barrow and take him away. He had never been known to walk. But now, on learning that the bank was about to collapse, Ganpat astonished everyone by leaping to his feet and actually running at a good speed in the direction of the bank. It soon became known that he had well over a thousand rupees in savings.

Men stood in groups at street corners, discussing the situation. There hadn't been so much excitement since India last won a Test match. The small town in the foothills seldom had a crisis, never had floods or earthquakes or droughts. And so the imminent crash of the local bank set everyone talking and speculating and rushing about in a frenzy.

Some boasted of their farsightedness, congratulating themselves on having taken out their money, or on never putting any in. Others speculated on the reasons for the crash, putting it all down to Seth Govind Ram's pleasure-loving ways. The Seth had fled the state, said one. He had fled the country, said another. He had a South American passport, said a third. Others insisted that he was hiding somewhere in the town. And there was a rumour that he had hanged himself from the tamarind tree, where he had been found that morning by the sweeper-boy.

Someone who had a relative working as a clerk in the bank decided to phone him and get the facts.

"I don't know anything about it," said the clerk, "except that half the town is here, trying to take their money out. Everyone seems to have gone mad!"

"There's a rumour that none of you have been paid."

"Well, all the clerks have had *their* salaries. We wouldn't be working otherwise. It may be that some of the part-time workers are getting paid late, but that isn't due to a shortage of money — only a few hundred rupees — it's just that the clerk who looks after their payments is on sick leave. You don't expect *me* to do his work, do you?" And he put the telephone down.

By afternoon the bank had gone through all its ready money, and the harassed manager was helpless. Emergency funds could only be obtained from one of the government banks, and now it was nearly closing time. He wasn't sure he could persuade the crowd outside to wait until the following morning. And Seth Govind Ram could be of no help from his luxury houseboat in Kashmir, five hundred miles away.

The clerks shut down their counters. But the people gathered outside on the steps of the bank, shouting: "We want our money!" "Give it to us today, or we'll break in!" "Fetch Seth Govind Ram, we know he's hiding in the vaults!"

Mischief-makers, who did not have a paisa in the bank, joined the crowd. The manager stood at the door and tried to calm his angry customers. He declared that the bank had plenty of money, that they could withdraw all they wanted the following morning.

"We want it now!" chanted the people. "Now, now, now!"

A few stones were thrown, and the manager retreated indoors, closing the iron-grille gate.

A brick hurtled through the air and smashed into the plate-glass window which advertised the bank's assets.

Then the police arrived. They climbed the steps of the bank and, using their long sticks, pushed the crowd back until people began falling over each other. Gradually everyone dispersed, shouting that they would be back in the morning.

Nathu arrived next morning to sweep the steps of the bank.

He saw the refuse and the broken glass and the stones cluttering up the steps. Raising his hands in horror, he cried: "Goondas! Hooligans! May they suffer from a thousand ills! It was bad enough being paid irregularly — now I must suffer an increase of work!" He smote the steps with his broom, scattering the refuse.

"Good morning, Nathu," said Sitaram, the washerman's son, getting down from his bicycle. "Are you ready to take up a new job from the first of next month? You'll have to, I suppose, now that the bank is closing."

"What did you say?" said Nathu.

"Haven't you heard? The bank's gone bankrupt. You'd better hang around until the others arrive, and then start

286

demanding your money too. You'll be lucky if you get it!"
He waved cheerfully, and pedalled away on his bicycle.

Nathu went back to sweeping the steps, muttering to himself. When he had finished, he sat down on the bottom step to await the arrival of the manager. He was determined to get his pay.

"Who would have thought the bank would collapse," he said to himself, and looked thoughtfully across the street. "I wonder how it could have happened ..."

Koki Plays the Game

"There's a cricket match on Saturday, isn't there?" asked Koki.

"That's right," said Ranji. "We're playing the Public School team."

"I might come and watch," said Koki.

"As you like. It won't be much of a game. We'll beat them easily."

Ranji's own cricket team was quite different from his school team. It consisted of boys big and small, long and short, from various walks of life. Even Koki, a girl, was allowed honorary membership, and had sometimes been 'twelfth man' — an extra. She knew the game well, and often bowled to Ranji in the mornings when he wanted batting practice. Only a couple of the team members could afford to go to private schools like Ranji's; most of them went to the local government school, and two or three had stopped going to school altogether.

There was Bhartu, who delivered newspapers in the mornings; the brothers Mukesh and Rakesh, whose father kept a sweet shop; and a tailor's son, Amir Ali.

288

There was Billy Jones, an Anglo-Indian boy; 'Lumboo' — the Tall One; Sitaram, the washerman's son, and several others. And there was also Bhim, who couldn't play at all, but who made a good umpire (when his glasses weren't steamed over) and who accompanied the team wherever it went.

This Saturday they were playing on their 'home' ground, a patch of wasteland behind a new cinema called the *Apsara* ('Heavenly Dancer').

The Public School boys had all arrived first, which was only natural since they lived together in the same boarding school. The members of Ranji's team came from different directions, so it was some time before they had all assembled. Even then they were two short. But Ranji won the toss and decided to bat, hoping that the missing team members would arrive in time to take their turn at the wicket.

"If Mukesh and Rakesh aren't here in time, we won't have them in the team," said Ranji sternly.

"Don't sack them," said Lumboo. "They always bring us sweets and snacks from their father's shop. We need them in the team even if they don't score any runs."

"Well, if they turn up *without* refreshments, they'll be sacked," said Ranji, always ready to be fair.

The two umpires had gone out to set up the stumps — Bhim, on behalf of Ranji's team, and a teacher from the Public School.

"I don't like the look of that teacher," said Amir Ali.

"Well, we won't take any risks."

Billy Jones and Lumboo always opened the batting.

289

Lumboo's height helped him to deal with the fast-rising ball. He took the first ball.

The Public School's opening bowler was speedy but inaccurate. This was because he was trying to bowl too fast. His first ball went for a wide, which gave Ranji's team its first run. The second ball wasn't quite so wide, but it was still about a foot from the leg stump. Lumboo took a swipe at it and missed. The third ball pitched half-way down the wicket and kept low. It struck Lumboo on the pads.

"How's that!" shouted the bowler, wicket-keeper and slip-fielders in unison.

The Public School's umpire did not hesitate. Up went his finger. Lumboo was given out leg-before-wicket.

Lumboo stood aghast. He looked down at where his feet were placed, then back at his stumps.

"I'm not in front of the wicket," he complained to no one in particular.

"The umpire's word is law," said the wicket-keeper.

Lumboo slowly walked back to where his teammates reclined against a pile of bricks.

"I wasn't out!" he protested.

"Never mind," said Ranji, whose turn it was to bat. "You'll get your chance when you come on to bowl."

He walked to the wicket with a confident air, his bat resting on his shoulder. He took guard carefully and, tapping his bat on the ground, faced the bowler. He received a straight ball, fast, and met it on the half-volley, driving it straight back past the bowler. It sped to the boundary, amidst delighted cries from Ranji's teammates. Four runs.

The next ball was short, just outside the off-stump. Ranji stepped back and square-cut it past point. Another four. There were more cheers, and this time Ranji distinctly heard a girl's voice shouting: "Good shot, Ranji!"

He looked back to where his teammates were gathered. There was no girl among them. He turned and looked towards the opposite boundary, and there, under the giant cinema hoarding, stood Koki. She waved to him.

Ranji did not wave back. He felt acutely self-conscious. Settling down to face the bowler again, he was aware of two things at once — of the bowler making faces and charging up to bowl, and of Koki standing on the boundary and waiting for him to hit another four. This loss of concentration caused him to misjudge the next ball. Instead of playing forward, he played back. The ball took the edge of his bat and flew straight into the wicket-keeper's gloves.

"How's that!" shouted all the fielders, appealing for a catch.

Ranji did not wait for the umpire — in this case, Bhim — to give him out. He knew he'd touched the ball. Scowling, he walked back to his team. It was all Koki's fault!

Now there was a good partnership between Sitaram and Bhartu. Sitaram, who helped his father with the town's washing on Sundays, was in the habit of laying out clothes on a flat stone and pounding them with a stout stick — the method followed by most washermen. He dealt with the cricket-ball in much the same way — clouting it hard, and

sending it to various points of the compass. He hit up twenty-five valuable runs before he was out, caught off a big hit. Bhartu pushed and prodded, merely keeping one end going, until he too was out to an LBW decision. Billy Jones had gone the same way, taking the ball on his pads. No one was happy with the LBW decisions.

"We must have neutral umpires," said Amir Ali.

"But who wants to be an umpire?" said Ranji. "We won't find anyone. We'll have to use our own team members — or let the other side provide *both* umpires!"

"Not after today," said Lumboo.

Meanwhile, Mukesh and Rakesh had arrived, carrying paper-bags full of samosas and jalebis. As a result, everyone cheered up. Wickets fell almost as rapidly as the snacks and sweets were consumed. Mukesh and Rakesh, who were the last men in, held out for several overs until Rakesh was given out — not really a match-winning score, except on a tricky wicket.

It was the Public School team's turn to bat. One of their opening batsmen was bowled by Lumboo for nought. The other batsman was twice rapped on the pads by balls from Ranji, but his loud appeals for LBW were turned down — by the Public School's umpire, naturally! Muttering to himself, Ranji hurled down a thunderbolt of a ball. It rose sharply and struck the batsman on the hand. Howling with pain, he dropped his bat and wrung his hand. Then he showed everyone a swollen finger and decided to 'retire hurt'.

"There's more than one way of getting them out," muttered Ranji, as he passed the umpire.

293

The next two batsmen were good players, not as nervous as the openers. One of them got what might have been a faint tickle to an out-swinger from Lumboo, but he was given the benefit of the doubt by Bhim — who, as umpires went, was as impartial as a star. He showed no favours to his own team, no matter what the other umpire did. It just isn't fair, thought Ranji.

The number three and four batsmen put on forty runs between them, and by mid-afternoon Ranji's players were feeling tired and hungry. Then three quick wickets fell to Sitaram's spinners. Three wickets remained, and twenty runs were needed by the Public School for victory.

This was when Bhartu, running to take a catch, collided with chubby Mukesh. Both of them went sprawling on the grass, and when they got up the ball was found lodged in the back of Mukesh's pants. How it got there no one could tell, but after much discussion the umpires had to agree that it qualified as a catch and the batsman was given out. But Bhartu had to leave the ground with a bleeding nose.

Ranji looked around for a replacement. There was no one in sight except Koki.

"Come and field," said Ranji brusquely.

Koki needed no persuading. She slipped off her sandals and dashed barefoot on to the field, taking up Bhartu's position near the boundary.

The tail-end batsmen were now swinging at the ball in a desperate attempt to hit off the remaining runs. A hard-hit drive sped past Koki and went for four runs. Ranji gave her a hard look. Then the two batsmen got into a muddle while trying to take a quick run, and one of them was run out.

The last man came in. The Public School was eight runs behind. But a couple of boundaries would take care of that.

The batsmen ran two. And then one of them, over-confident and sure of victory, swung out at a slow, tempting ball from Sitaram, and the ball flew towards Koki in a long, curving arc.

Koki had to run a few yards to her left. Then she leapt like a gazelle and took the ball in both hands.

Ranji's team had won, and Koki had made the winning catch.

It was her last appearance as 'twelfth man'. From that day onwards she was a regular member of the team.

"The boy's useless," said Mr Kapoor, speaking to his wife but making sure his son could hear. "I don't know what he'll do with himself when he grows up. He takes no interest in his studies."

Suraj's father had returned from a business trip and was seeing his son's school report for the first time.

"Good at cricket," said the report. "Poor in studies. Does not pay attention in class."

Suraj's mother, a quiet, dignified woman, said nothing. Suraj stood at the window, refusing to speak. He stared out at the light drizzle that whispered across the garden. He had angry black eyes and bushy eyebrows, and he was feeling rebellious.

His father was doing all the talking. "What's the use of spending money on his education if he can't show anything for it? He comes home, eats as much as three boys, asks for money, and then goes out to loaf with his friends!"

Mr Kapoor paused, expecting Suraj to reply and give cause for further scolding; but Suraj knew that silence would irritate his father even more, and there were times when he enjoyed watching his father get irritated.

"Well, I won't stand for it," said Mr Kapoor finally.

"If you don't make some effort, my boy, you can leave this house!" And having at last addressed Suraj directly, he stormed out of the room.

Suraj remained a few moments at the window. Then he went to the front door, opened it, stepped out into the rain, and banged the door behind him.

His mother made as if to call out after him, but she thought better of it, and turned and walked into the kitchen.

Suraj stood in the drizzle, looking back at the house.

"I'll never go back," he said fiercely. "I can manage without them. If they want me back, they can come and *ask* me to return!"

And he thrust his hands into his pockets and walked down the road with an independent air.

His fingers came into contact with a familiar crispness, a five-rupee note. It was all the money he had in the world. He clutched it tight. He had meant to spend it at the cinema, but now it would have to serve more urgent needs. He wasn't sure what these needs would be because just now he was angry and his mind wasn't running on practical lines. He walked blindly, unconscious of the rain, until he reached the maidaan.

When he reached the maidaan, the sun came out.

Though there was still a drizzle, the sun seemed to raise Suraj's spirits at once. He remembered his friend Ranji and decided he would stay with Ranji until he found some sort of work. He knew that if he didn't find work, he wouldn't be able to stay away from home for long. He wondered what kind of work a thirteen-year-old could get. He did not fancy delivering newspapers or serving tea in a small teashop in the bazaar; it was much better being a customer.

The drizzle ceased altogether, and Suraj hurried across the maidaan and down a quiet road until he reached Ranji's house. When he went in at the gate, his spirits sank.

The house was shut. There was a lock on the front door. Suraj went round the house three times but he couldn't find an open door or window. Perhaps, he thought, the family have gone out for the morning — a picnic or birthday treat; they were sure to be back for lunch. With spirits mounting once again, he strolled leisurely down the road, in the direction of the bazaar.

Suraj had a weakness for the bazaar, for its crowded variety of goods, its smells and colours and the music playing over the loudspeakers. He lingered now at a tea-and-pakora shop, tempted by the appetising smells that came from inside; but decided that he would eat at Ranji's house and spend his money on something other than food. He couldn't resist the big yellow yo-yo in the toy-seller's glass case; it was set with pieces of different coloured glass which shone and twinkled in the sunshine.

"How much?" asked Suraj.

"Two rupees," said the shopkeeper. "But to a regular customer like you I give it for one rupee."

"It must be an old one," said Suraj, but he paid the

298

rupee and took possession of the yo-yo. He immediately began working it, strolling through the bazaar with the yo-yo swinging up and down from his index finger.

Fingering the four remaining notes in his pocket, he decided that he was thirsty. Not tap-water, nor a fizzy drink, but only a vanilla milk-shake would meet his need. He sat at a table and sucked milk-shake through a straw. One eye caught sight of the clock on the wall. It was nearly one o'clock. Ranji and his family should be home by now.

Suraj slipped off his chair, paid for the drink — that left him with two rupees — and went sauntering down the bazaar road, the yo-yo making soothing sounds beside him.

Ranji's house was still shut.

This was something Suraj hadn't anticipated. He walked quickly round the house, but it was locked as before. On his second round he met the gardener, an old man over sixty.

"Where is everybody?" asked Suraj.

"They have gone to Delhi for a week," said the gardener, looking sharply at Suraj. "Why, is anything the matter?"

Suraj had never seen the old man before, but he did not hesitate to confide in him. "I've left home. I was going to stay with Ranji. Now there's nowhere to go."

The old man thought this over for a minute. His face was wrinkled like a walnut, his hands and feet hard and cracked; but his eyes were bright and almost youthful. He was a part-time gardener, who worked for several families along the road; there were no big gardens in this part of the town.

"Why don't you go home again?" he suggested.

"It's too soon," said Suraj. "I haven't really run away as yet. They must *know* I've run away. Then they'll feel sorry!"

The gardener smiled. "You should have planned it better," he said. "Have you saved any money?"

"I had five rupees this morning. Now there are two rupees left." He looked down at his yo-yo. "Would you like to buy it?"

"I wouldn't know how to work it," said the gardener. "The best thing for you to do is to go home, wait till Ranji gets back, and *then* run away."

Suraj considered this interesting advice, and decided that there was something in it. But he didn't make up his mind right away. A little suspense at home would be a good thing for his parents.

He returned to the maidaan and sat down on the grass. As soon as he sat down, he felt hungry.

He had never felt so hungry before. Visions of tandoori chickens and dripping spangled sweets danced before him. He wondered if the toy-seller would take back the yo-yo. He probably would, for half the price; but, as much as Suraj wanted food, he did not want to give up the yo-yo.

There was nothing to do but go home. His mother, he was sure, would be worried by now. His father (he hoped) would be pacing up and down the verandah, glancing at his watch every few seconds. It would be a lesson to them. He would walk back into the house as if doing them a favour.

He only hoped they had kept his lunch.

Suraj walked into the sitting-room and threw his yo-yo on the sofa.

Mr Kapoor was sitting in his favourite armchair, reading a newspaper prior to going back to his office. He stood up for a moment as Suraj came into the room, said "You 're very late," and returned to his newspaper.

Suraj found his mother and his food in the kitchen. She did not speak to him, but was smiling to herself.

"Feeling hungry?" she asked.

"No," said Suraj, and seized the tray and tucked into his food.

When he returned to the sitting-room he was surprised to see his father fumbling with the yo-yo.

"How do you work this stupid thing?" said Mr Kapoor.

Suraj didn't reply. He just stood there gloating over his father's clumsiness. At last he couldn't help bursting into laughter.

"It's easy," he said. "I'll show you." And he took the yo-yo from his father and gave a demonstration.

When Mrs Kapoor came into the room she did not appear at all surprised to find her husband and son deeply absorbed in the working of a cheap bazaar toy. She was used to such absurdities. Men never really grew up.

Mr Kapoor had forgotten he was supposed to be returning to his office, and Suraj had forgotten about running away. They had both forgotten the morning's unpleasantness. That had been a long, long time ago.

The Visitor

Amir was sitting on his bed, staring out of the door that opened out onto the roof. The bald mynah bird stared back at him. Then he heard someone calling from downstairs.

"Does anyone live up there?"

"No," shouted Amir. "Nobody lives up here."

"Then can I come up?" asked the person below.

Amir didn't answer. Presently he heard footsteps coming up. The mynah bird flew off the roof and settled in a mango tree.

A boy stood in the doorway, smiling at Amir. He was a little taller than Amir, and much thinner. He wore a white shirt outside striped pyjamas. On his feet were open slippers. A tray hung from his shoulders, filled with an assortment of goods.

"Would you like to buy something?" he asked.

In his tray were combs, buttons, reels of thread, shoelaces, little vials of cheap perfume.

"I have everything you need," he said.

"I don't need anything," said Amir.

"You need buttons."

"I don't."

"Your top button is missing."

Amir felt for the top button of his shirt and was surprised to find it missing.

"I don't like buttoning my shirt," he said.

"That's different," said his visitor, and looked him up and down for further signs of wear and tear. "You'd better buy a new pair of shoelaces."

Amir looked down at his shoes and said, "I've got laces."

"Very poor quality," said the boy, and taking hold of one of the laces, he tugged at it and snapped it in two. "See how easily it breaks? Now you need laces."

"Well, I'm not buying any," said Amir.

The boy sighed, shrugged, and moved towards the door. As he walked slowly down the steps, Amir stood in the doorway, watching him go. On an impulse, he called out, "What's your name?"

"Mohan," replied the boy.

"Well, come again in a week," said Amir. "I may need something then."

Amir went downstairs for his lunch. He returned to his room to study, but dozed off instead. Towards evening he felt hungry and restless. He could not remain in his room when everyone else was pouring into the streets to shop and talk and eat and visit the cinema.

From the roof he could see the bazaar lights coming on, and hear the jingle of tonga bells and the blare of bus

303

horns. It was a cool evening and he put on his coat before going downstairs.

It was not easy to walk fast on the road to the bazaar. Apart from the great number of pedestrians, there were cyclists and scooter-rickshaws, handcarts and cows, all making movement difficult. A little tea-shop played film music over a loudspeaker, adding noise to the general confusion.

The balloon-man was having a trying time. He was surrounded by a swarm of children who were more intent on bursting his balloons than on buying any. One or two got loose and went sailing over the heads of the crowd to burst over the fire in the chaat shop.

Amir stood outside the chaat shop and ate a variety of spicy snacks. Then he wiped his fingers on the banana leaves on which he had been served, and moved on down the bazaar road.

Towards the clock tower the road grew wider and less crowded. There was a street lamp at the corner of the road. A boy was sitting on the pavement beneath the lamp, bent over a book, absorbed in what he was reading. He seemed not to notice the noise of the bazaar or the chill in the air. As Amir came nearer, he saw that the boy was Mohan.

He did not know whether to stop and talk to him, or carry on down the road. After walking some distance, he felt ashamed at not having stopped to greet the boy, so he turned and retraced his steps. But when he came to the lamp-post, Mohan had gone.

*

When Mohan came again he did not call out from below but came straight up to the room. He looked at Amir's shirt and shoes and saw that one of the shoes was still done up with half a lace. With an air of triumph he dropped a pair of shoelaces on the desk.

"I can't pay for them now," said Amir.

"You can pay me later."

Amir sat on the edge of his table while Mohan leant against the wall.

"Do you go to school?" asked Amir.

"Sometimes I go to evening classes," Mohan said. "I am sitting privately for my High School exams next month. If I pass..."

He stopped to think about the things he could do if he passed. The way to a career would be open to him, he could study further, become an engineer, or a scientist or an administrator. No more selling combs and buttons at street corners...

"Where are your parents?" asked Amir.

"My father is dead. My mother is in our village in the hills. I have brothers and sisters at home, but I am the only one old enough to work."

"Then where do you stay?"

"Anywhere. On somebody's verandah, or on the maidaan; it doesn't matter much in the summer. These days I sleep on the station platform. It's quite warm there."

"You can sleep here," said Amir.

One morning, when he opened the door of his room, Amir found Mohan asleep at the top of the steps. He had

305

wrapped himself up in a thin blanket. His tray of merchandise lay a short distance away.

Amir shook him gently and he woke up immediately, blinking in the bright sunlight.

"Why didn't you come in?" asked Amir. "Why didn't you let me know you were here?"

"It was late," said Mohan. "I did not want to wake you. Besides, it was a fine night, not too cold."

"Someone could have stolen your things."

Amir made Mohan promise to sleep in the room that night. He came quite early. Amir lent him another blanket, and he lay down on the floor-mat and slept soundly, while Amir stayed awake worrying if his guest was comfortable enough.

Mohan came quite often, leaving early in the morning before Amir could offer him a meal. He ate at little places in the bazaar.

The High School exams were nearing, and Mohan sat up late with his books. Apart from his occasional evening classes, he received no teaching.

The exams lasted for ten days, and during this time Mohan put aside his tray of odds and ends. He did his papers with confidence. He thought he had done rather well. And when it was over, he took up his tray again and walked all over the town, trying to make up for lost sales.

On the day the exam results were due, Amir rose early. He got to the news agency at five o'clock, just as the morning papers arrived. Bhartu gave him a paper to look at and he found the page on which the results were listed.

306

He looked down the 'passes' column for the town, but couldn't find Mohan's number on the list. He looked twice to make sure, and then returned the paper to Bhartu with a glum look.

"Failed?" said Bhartu.

Amir nodded and turned away. When he returned to the room, he found Mohan sitting at the top of the steps. He didn't have to tell him anything. Mohan knew by the look on the other's face.

Amir sat down beside him, and they said nothing for a while.

"Never mind," said Mohan. "I'll pass next year." It seemed that Amir was more in need of comforting than himself.

"If only you'd had more time," said Amir.

"I have plenty of time now. Another year... Can I still stay in your room?"

"For as long as it's my room. That means I shall have to work too, otherwise my grandfather will drag me downstairs again."

Mohan laughed and went into the room. When he came out, the tray was hanging from his shoulders.

"What would you like to buy?" he asked. "I have everything you need."

Mukesh Keeps a Goat

Mukesh's favourite pet was the little black goat who followed him home from the mustard fields one day.

Each year, before the monsoon rains came, the little Song River outside Dehra was just a narrow stream. Mukesh liked wading across it and then wandering through the fields and tea gardens on the other side, watching the men moving about among the yellow mustard and the women in their bright red saris picking tea.

He had been sitting on the bank of a small irrigation canal, gazing at a couple of herons fishing in the muddy water, when he felt something bump his elbow. Looking around, he found at his side a little goat, jet black and soft as velvet, with lovely grey eyes. Neither her owner nor her mother was around.

She continued to nudge Mukesh, so he looked in his pockets for nourishment and, finding the remains of a samosa, held it out to her. She ate it eagerly, then sat down beside him and began nibbling at the grass.

A little later, when Mukesh got up to leave, the goat rose too. And when he started walking home, she followed unsteadily, her thin legs taking her this way and that.

"Go home!" said Mukesh as she danced around him. But it was clear that she had forgotten the way home, because she followed him to the river-bed. It was obvious that her trembling legs would not stand up to the current, so he took her in his arms and carried her across the stream. When he set her down, she remained by his side, rubbing against his legs.

Mukesh set out for home at a brisk pace, feeling sure that he would soon leave the little goat behind. But her legs were stronger than he had supposed. She came hopping along, right up to the gate of the house.

There was nothing he could do but carry her in and present her to his parents. "She's my friend," he announced.

"Not another pet!" said his mother when she saw the goat on the verandah, lapping a saucer of milk. "I've told you again and again that I will not have any animals in or around the house!"

It was easy to understand his mother's objections. Only a few weeks previously Mukesh had started his own zoo in the back garden. As a result, their neighbours' parrot, borrowed and put on display, had escaped; the washerman's donkey had gone missing for two days; and Mukesh's mother had found her kitchen full of fleeing lizards.

"And besides," she said, "your dog won't be happy with a goat in the house."

But Mukesh's black dog (with yellow eyes) merely

looked up from the bone he was gnawing at the other end of the verandah, and paid no attention to the newcomer. There would be no competition from a grass-eater who could not dig for bones!

"Goat's milk is good for your health," said Mukesh. "I read about it somewhere. That's why I brought her home. You haven't been looking well this week, Mother."

The prospect of an eventual supply of free milk tilted the decision in favour of keeping the goat, even though they knew it would be some time before it would provide any. Mukesh's little sister Dolly did not think highly of the new pet. "It *smells*," was all she said, when asked her opinion. So Mukesh gave his pet a liberal sprinkling of his mother's jasmine perfume, with the result that she reeked of perfume for a week.

But there was something fairy-like about the little goat, and Mukesh named her Pari, meaning 'fairy'. She skipped about very daintily, and her feet seemed equipped with springs when she leaped around the small lawn. To make the name even more fitting, Mukesh tied a little bell to her neck so he'd always know by its fairy tinkling where she was.

She loved an early-morning walk and was in many ways as good or even a better companion than a dog: she did not wander off on her own or get into quarrels with cows, cats, stray dogs, or porcupines. The only things she chased were butterflies, and she would tumble into ditches and slither down slopes in her eagerness to follow them.

But unlike fairies, who never grow up, Mukesh's Pari

310

had to grow up, and she soon developed a neat little pair of horns. Her appetite began to increase, too. She loved the leaves and flowers of the sweet-pea, the nasturtium and the geranium. These were also Mukesh's father's favourite garden flowers! It was he, rather than Mukesh's mother, who loved growing flowers, and every year his sweet-peas won prizes at the annual Flower Show.

One morning he found most of his sweet-peas destroyed. Hastily Mukesh blamed a cow, suggesting that it had got into the garden during the night. His father made no comment, but gave him a look that suggested he knew just who the culprit was; it was obvious that he bitterly regretted having allowed Mukesh to keep the goat. By the time the Flower Show came around, he had only his zinnias left — apparently the goat disliked zinnias — and they won third prize. Mukesh took care to keep the goat well out of his father's sight.

Of course, trouble, just like unseasonal rain, came when Mukesh was least expecting it.

Pari, having discovered various uses to which she could put her horns, began trying them out at almost every opportunity. A part-time gardener, who had never been known to grumble, came to Mukesh's mother to complain that he had been bending over the sweet-pea bed, putting it right again, when the goat had come up quietly and butted him from behind. He refused to work in the garden unless Pari was tied up.

"And by the way," said Mukesh's mother to her son, after she had been calmed down, "when are we going to have that milk we were promised?"

It wasn't long before the postman, the fruit-seller and the newspaper boy all had complaints to make. They dared not turn their backs on the playful young goat.

Events reached a climax during the visit of one of Mukesh's aunts. Chachi (his uncle's wife) was in a habit of bending over flower-pots and holding brief conversations with the flowers. She said it helped them grow faster.

She was poised over a pot, talking to a geranium, when the goat, suspecting that Chachi was eating the leaves, decided to butt this intruder out of the way of her favourite snack.

Chachi did not take kindly to being pushed off the verandah. She insisted that she had been badly bruised, though she refused all offers of first-aid from Mukesh.

It was the end of the goat's comfortable stay with the family. Mukesh's father asked Nathu, the newspaper boy, to take her straight to the bazaar and sell her at any price to the first customer that came along.

Mukesh stood at the gate and watched his Pari being led away. She kept looking back and bleating, probably wondering why Mukesh was not accompanying her on this particular walk.

Nathu gave Mukesh a smile and a wink, as if to suggest that all would be well. Nathu had worked as a cleaner at a local co-op bank before it had collapsed; now he sold newspapers; but his 'banking experience', as he put it, had made him a good judge of a promising investment. When he came back from the bazaar, he announced that the goat had been sold, and handed Mukesh's father a fifty-rupee note. But later, when he was alone with Mukesh, he told him that he had bought the goat himself, and that Mukesh could come and see her from time to time in her new home behind the bazaar.

Mukesh did visit her sometimes. And in due course he found her with a little kid. Pari had also become a good provider of milk, and Nathu and his small brothers and sisters were great milk drinkers. She was on good terms with everyone in the family and only butted strangers who bowed too low when entering or leaving by the small courtyard door.

Koki's Song

When Koki was nearly twelve, she and her mother went to spend part of the year with Koki's maternal grandmother who lived in a lonely old house near the river-bed. Her mother was busy all day, cooking and washing clothes, while her grandmother, a round, bouncy little woman, would sit in the sun recounting stories from her own childhood.

Koki would spend the morning helping her mother and the afternoons talking to her grandmother. Towards evening the old lady would go indoors, and then Koki would be on her own in the large garden.

The garden had not been looked after too well, and it was over-run with semi-wild marigolds, nasturtiums and roses. Koki liked it this way because she could wander about discovering flowers emerging from tall grass and thistles. A wall went round the garden, and on the other side of the wall a stretch of grassland went sloping down to the river-bed. A shallow stream ran along the middle of this otherwise dry watercourse. During the monsoon rains it was a rushing torrent, but just now it was a murmuring brook, with little silver fish darting about in the water.

Koki seldom went beyond the garden wall because across the river-bed was jungle, and wild animals frequently came down to the water to drink. The wild boar, who were often seen, frightened her. But once she saw a deer, quite close, moving about with supple grace and dignity. It was a chital, a spotted deer. Koki stared at the animal in fascination, and the deer must have become conscious of her gaze, for it looked up and stared back at Koki. What the deer saw was a small dark face, half-hidden by a lot of loose black hair, and two large brown eyes shining with wonder.

The deer and the girl stared at each other for two or three minutes, then somewhere a twig snapped and the startled deer went bounding away across the stream.

One evening Koki heard the distant music of a flute. She had not heard it before, and she looked over the wall to see where it came from.

A boy sat near the stream, playing on a flute, while his small herd of cows grazed on the slopes. He had a thin shawl thrown over his shoulders, his feet were bare, and his clothes dusty and torn. But Koki did not notice these things; she was enthralled by the simple, plaintive melody of the flute and, for her, the boy was a prince who made beautiful music.

She climbed up on the wall and sat there with her legs dangling over the other side. When the boy looked up and saw her, he rose and came nearer. He sat down on the grass about twenty metres from the wall, put the flute

315

to his lips again and, with his eyes on Koki, continued his playing.

It reminded Koki of the day she and the deer had stared at each other, both fascinated, neither of them stirring or making a sound; only now it was for a much longer time, and one played while the other listened.

Next evening, Koki heard the flute again and was soon sitting astride the wall. When the boy saw Koki, he put down his flute and smiled at her, and then began playing again. That evening, besides playing and listening, all they did was smile at each other.

On the third evening Koki asked the boy his name. "Somi," he said, and he played on the flute and did not say another word.

But on the fourth evening he asked Koki her name, and she told him.

"I will make a song about you," he said, and he played the sweetest melody Koki had ever heard. She found herself putting words to it and singing softly:

"When you are far away,
I'll sing this song,
And in my heart you'll play
All summer long."

After that, Somi always played Koki's song.

It wasn't long before Koki came down from the wall, and sometimes she and Somi would walk up the river-bed and paddle in the cold mountain water. They never said much to each other, and yet a lot seemed to have been said. Somi would leave at dusk, herding the cattle before him, calling each by a different name, and Koki would

316

watch him go until he was a speck on the dusty road and the cow-bells tinkled distantly. She never knew where he came from or where he went. She thought she might ask him some day, but it didn't seem necessary.

One day Somi did not play the flute. Instead he put it in Koki's hands and said, "Keep it for me, I am going away for some time. To the summer pastures in the hills." He had come without his herd that day and, after he had given Koki the flute, he turned and ran fleet-footed across the grass that was now turning from green to brown.

Koki missed the boy, but she still had the flute. She tried playing on it sometimes, but she did not have the magic touch and all she achieved was a shrill, broken piping. But sometimes, when she was walking by herself along the dry river-bed, she thought she heard the music, sweet and low and all around her. She did not sing her song. She had made the words for Somi, and she would sing them for Somi when he returned — if ever he returned...

At night, when she lay awake, the flute seemed to play her song. It was as though the flute was actually playing by itself.

One day when Koki was at the river-bed, ankle-deep in water, the flute fell from her hands. It was carried into the middle of the stream and swept away. Koki ran downstream, splashing through the water, stumbling frequently and wetting her clothes. She could see the flute bobbing up and down on the water, but it was getting further and further away, and soon she had to stop running because she was tired and far from home.

The flute was lost, and she did not hear its music any more.

Koki became quiet and listless. Grandmother complained that she could no longer interest the girl in her stories, so Koki tried hard to listen and pay attention, but her mind was always wandering to other things. No one really knew the reason for Koki's unhappiness; even Koki wasn't sure. Grandmother had of course seen Koki and the boy talking to each other but did not realise the strength of the bond between them.

Koki saw the deer once, when it came to the stream to drink. She was sitting on the wall, and the deer took one look at her and was so startled that it went bounding away into the forest.

And so another month passed. The mountain snows melted and the swollen stream came rushing down the valley and past the lonely old house. The garden was full of little green shoots, the grass was fresh and sweet, and the flame-tree was bursting into colour. Koki had grown a little taller, too.

She sat under a mango tree, watching the sunlight stalk the shadows on the wall. A couple of bulbuls were twittering away in a rose bush. Grandmother had told Koki that birds sang because they were happy, but what proof was there of that, Koki wondered? For all she knew, birds could just as well be singing because they felt miserable.

And then, as though accompanying the song of the birds, came the music of a flute.

Koki heard it, and looked up and listened. There was no mistaking the melody. It was Koki's song. She pulled herself up on the wall and looked over.

Somi sat on the grass, playing a new flute, but looking as though he had been sitting there for ages. When he saw Koki, he put down his flute and smiled, and then began playing again.

That evening they walked together down to the edge of the stream, and she noticed that the herd was larger than before. Somi was wearing new clothes. He told her about the lush mountain meadow where he had taken the herd for the dry month; she told him that she would soon be returning to her school and home in the nearby town.

"Will you come again?" he asked.

"At the end of every month," she said. "My grandmother says I must come." But she knew that wasn't the only reason.

"I'll be here," said Somi simply, and played her song. And Koki sang to his music.

The Great Train Journey

Suraj waved to a passing train, and kept waving until only the spiralling smoke remained. He liked waving to trains. He wondered about the people in them, and about where they were going and what it would be like there. And when the train had passed, leaving behind only the hot, empty track, Suraj was lonely.

He was a little lonely now. His hands in his pockets, he wandered along the railway track, kicking at loose pebbles and sending them down the bank. Soon there were other tracks, a railway-siding, a stationary goods train.

Suraj walked the length of the goods train. The carriage doors were closed and, as there were no windows, he couldn't see inside. He looked around to see if he was observed, and then, satisfied that he was alone, began trying the doors. He was almost at the end of the train when a carriage door gave way to his thrust.

It was dark inside the carriage. Suraj stood outside in the bright sunlight, peering into the darkness, trying to recognise bulky, shapeless objects. He stepped into the carriage and felt around. The objects were crates, and through the cross-section of woodwork he felt straw. He opened the other door and the sun streamed into the compartment, driving out the musty darkness.

Suraj sat down on a packing-case, his chin cupped in his hands. The school was closed for the summer holidays, and he had been wandering about all day and still did not know what to do with himself. The carriage was bare of any sort of glamour. Passing trains fascinated him — moving trains, crowded trains, shrieking, panting trains all fascinated him — but this smelly, dark compartment filled him only with gloom and more loneliness.

He did not really look gloomy or lonely. He looked fierce at times, when he glared out at people from under his dark eyebrows, but otherwise he usually wore a contented look — and no one could guess just how deep his thoughts were!

Perhaps, if he had company, some fun could be had in the carriage. If there had been a friend with him, someone like Ranji ....

He looked at the crates. He was always curious about things that were bolted or nailed down or in some way concealed from him — things like parcels and locked rooms — and carriage doors and crates!

He went from one crate to another, and soon his perseverance was rewarded. The cover of one hadn't been properly nailed down. Suraj got his fingers under the edge and prised up the lid. Absorbed in this operation, he did not notice the slight shudder that passed through the train.

He plunged his hands into the straw and pulled out

321

an apple.

It was a dark, ruby-red apple, and it lay in the dusty palm of Suraj's hand like some gigantic precious stone, smooth and round and glowing in the sunlight. Suraj looked up, out of the doorway, and thought he saw a tree walking past the train.

He dropped the apple and stared.

There was another tree, and another, all walking past the door with increasing rapidity. Suraj stepped forward but lost his balance and fell on his hands and knees. The floor beneath him was vibrating, the wheels were clattering on the rails, the carriage was swaying. The trees were running now, swooping past the train, and the telegraph poles joined them in the crazy race.

Crouching on his hands and knees, Suraj stared out of the open door and realised that the train was moving, moving fast, moving away from his home and puffing into the unknown. He crept cautiously to the door and looked out. The ground seemed to rush away from the wheels. He couldn't jump. Was there, he wondered, any way of stopping the train? He looked around the compartment again: only crates of apples. He wouldn't starve, that was one consolation.

He picked up the apple he had dropped and pulled a crate nearer to the doorway. Sitting down, he took a bite from the apple and stared out of the open door.

"Greetings, friend," said a voice from behind, and Suraj spun round guiltily, his mouth full of apple.

A dirty, bearded face was looking out at him from behind a pile of crates. The mouth was open in a wide,

322

paan-stained grin.

"Er — namaste," said Suraj apprehensively. "Who are you?"

The man stepped out from behind the crates and confronted the boy.

"I'll have one of those, too," he said, pointing to the apple.

Suraj gave the man an apple, and stood his ground while the carriage rocked on the rails. The man took a step forward, lost his balance, and sat down on the floor.

"And where are you going, friend?" he asked. "Have you a ticket?"

"No," said Suraj. "Have you?"

The man pulled at his beard and mused upon the question but did not answer it. He took a bite from the apple and said, "No, I don't have a ticket. But I usually reserve this compartment for myself. This is the first time I've had company. Where are you going? Are you a hippy like me?"

"I don't know," said Suraj. "Where does this train go?"

The scruffy ticketless traveller looked concerned for a moment, then smiled and said, "Where do you want to go?"

"I want to go everywhere," said Suraj. "I want to go to England and China and Africa and Greenland. I want to go all over the world!"

"Then you're on the right train," said the man. "This train goes everywhere. First it will take you to the sea, and there you will have to get on a ship if you want to go to China."

"How do I get on a ship?" asked Suraj.

The man, who had been fumbling about in the folds and pocket of his shabby clothes, produced a packet of bidis and a box of matches, and began smoking the aromatic leaf.

"Can you cook?" he asked.

"Yes," said Suraj untruthfully.

"Can you scrub a deck?"

"Why not?"

"Can you sail a ship?"

"I can sail anything."

"Then you'll get to China," said the man.

He leant back against a crate, stuck his dirty feet up on another crate, and puffed contentedly at his bidi.

Suraj finished his apple, took another from the crate, and dug his teeth into it. He took aim with the core of the old apple and tried to hit a telegraph pole, but missed it by metres; it wasn't the same as throwing a cricket ball. Then, to make the apple more interesting, he began to take big bites to see if he could devour it in three mouthfuls. But it took him four bites to finish the apple, so he started on another.

Suraj had always wanted to be in a train, a train that would take him to strange new places, over hundreds and hundreds of kilometres. And here was a train doing just that, and he wasn't quite sure if it was what he really wanted... .

The train was coming to a station. The engine whistled, slowed down. The number of railway lines increased, crossed, spread out in different directions. Before the train could come to a stop, Suraj's companion came to the door and jumped to the ground.

"You'd better keep out of sight if you don't want to be caught!" he called. And waving his hand, he disappeared into the jungle across the railway tracks.

The train was at a siding. Suraj couldn't see any signs of life, but he heard voices and the sound of carriage doors being opened and closed. He suspected that the apples wouldn't stay in the compartment much longer, so he stuffed one into each pocket, and climbed on to a wooden rack in a corner.

Presently men's voices were heard in the doorway. Two labourers stepped into the compartment and began moving the crates towards the door, where they were taken over by others. Soon the compartment was empty.

Suraj waited until the men had gone away before coming down from the rack. After about five minutes the train started again. It shunted up and down, then gathered speed and went rushing across the plain.

Suraj felt a thrill of anticipation. Where would they be going now? He wondered what his parents would do when he failed to come home that night; they would think he had run away, or been kidnapped, or been involved in an accident. They would have the police out and there would be search parties. Suraj would be famous: the boy who disappeared!

The train came out of the jungle and passed fields of sugarcane and villages of mud huts. Children shouted and waved to the train, though there was no one in it except Suraj, the guard and the engine-driver. Suraj waved back. Usually he was in a field, waving; today, he was actually on the train.

He was beginning to enjoy the ride. The train would take him to the sea. There would be ships with funnels and ships with sails, and there might even be one to take him across the ocean to some distant land. He felt a bit sorry for his mother and father — they *would* miss him ... they would believe he had been lost for ever... ! But one day, a fortune made, he would return home and then nobody would care any more about school reports and what he ate and why he came home late... Ranji would be waiting for him at the station, and Suraj would bring him back a present — an African lion, perhaps, or a transistor-radio... But he wished Ranji was with him now; he wished the ragged hippy was still with him. An adventure was always more fun when one had company.

He had finished both apples by the time the train showed signs of reaching another station. This time it seemed to be moving into the station itself, not just a siding. It passed a lot of signals and buildings and advertisement-boards before slowing to a halt beside a wide, familiar platform.

Suraj looked out of the door and caught sight of the board bearing the station's name. He was so astonished that he almost fell out of the compartment. He was back in his home town! After travelling forty or fifty kilometres, here he was, home again.

He couldn't understand it. The train hadn't turned, of that he was certain; and it hadn't been moving backwards, he was certain of that, too. He climbed out of the compartment and looked up and down the platform. Yes, the engine had changed ends! It was only the local apple train.

Suraj glowered angrily at everyone on the platform. It was as though the rest of the world had played a trick on him.

He made his way to the waiting-room and slipped into the street through the back door. He did not want a ticket-collector asking him awkward questions. It had been a free ride, and with that he comforted himself. Shrugging his shoulders, Suraj sauntered down the road to the bazaar. Some day, he thought, he'd take a train and really go somewhere; and he'd buy a ticket, just to make sure of getting there.

"I'm going everywhere," he said fiercely. "I'm going everywhere, and no one can stop me!"